Spell Found

(Blackmoore Sisters Cozy Mystery Series Book 7)

Leighann Dobbs

This is a work of fiction.

None of it is real. All names, places, and events are products of the author's imagination. Any resemblance to real names, places, or events are purely coincidental, and should not be construed as being real.

Chapter 1

Crystals and gemstones of all shapes and sizes glittered in a dazzling array of color from atop their black velvet cushions inside the countertop display case. The sheer assortment would have made it difficult for most people to single out one stone in particular, but Fiona Blackmoore knew exactly which one she was interested in. *That* stone was an odd rectangular shape, smaller at the bottom than at the top, and it glowed in a rainbow of red and purple hues.

Mesmerized by its beauty, Fiona pushed a long tendril of her curly red hair behind her shoulder as she bent down to get a closer look at the unusual stone. A slight breeze caressed her face. The melodic tinkling of wind chimes and a whiff of jasmine-scented incense reminded her of where she was—inside a small shop called *Eye of Newt* in Freeport, Maine.

Outside, tourists strolled past the shop, colorful bags dangling from their arms, round sunglasses perched on their noses, some of them wearing wide-brimmed hats to shield them from the harsh June sun.

Inside, the shop was quiet. No other customers browsed among the colorful tarot cards, mystical statues, essential oils, candles and crystals. That was just as well since Fiona and her sister Morgan weren't there to shop like tourists. They had an important job to do.

Fiona pointed at the gemstone, causing the other stones and crystals in the case to brighten as her hand passed over them. "This is the stone, the one we've been looking for. No wonder you had a feeling we should come here."

Though the girls owned their own shop, *Sticks and Stones,* In Noquitt, Maine, where Morgan mixed up potent herbal remedies and Fiona designed healing crystal jewelry, they sometimes worked assignments for a paranormal security agency. They suspected their employers were actually a secret department in Homeland Security. They'd been called into service some years earlier after The Agency discovered the girls' unique paranormal gifts, gifts that The Agency convinced them were important weapons in the fight to quell the rising tide of negative and dark energy in the world.

After receiving a cryptic note from The Agency a few months earlier, Fiona, Morgan and their two sisters had been on the hunt for an unusual gemstone. They'd spent countless hours scouring antique shops and mystical shops as well as following up on leads. When Morgan's intuition —her unique paranormal gift the girls had learned to respect and value highly—had led them to *Eye of Newt*, Fiona suspected they might be on to something.

Morgan's long, jet-black hair brushed the top of the case as she bent over to get a closer look. "Well, it sure is acting special." Morgan narrowed her ice blue eyes and moved her face closer to the case. "But it's not shaped like a key."

"Not the kind of key you open a door with, but a key*stone*. You know, the wedge-shaped stone at the top of a stone archway. I guess we made an erroneous assumption about the shape when we read the note."

"*Meow!*"

A fluffy black cat hopped silently onto the top of the display case and sashayed down its length, flicking her luxurious tail in Morgan's then Fiona's face.

"I think we need to buy this." Fiona scratched the cat behind the ears, then bent down to feline eye level. "Go get your human. We have a purchase to make."

The cat regarded Fiona suspiciously through slitted, golden eyes.

"Where is the shop owner, anyway?" Morgan glanced at a black curtain hanging in a doorway at the back of the shop.

"*Meow*!" The cat hopped down from the case and disappeared behind the curtain.

A second later, the curtain parted and a woman came out. Fiona judged her to be in her late twenties, about the same age as Fiona and Morgan. The woman was an exotic beauty with a flawless olive complexion and a wavy cascade of long, mink brown hair that fell to her waist.

"Welcome to *Eye of Newt*. I'm Cassiopeia. Can I help you?" Her golden brown eyes seemed to glow as they skipped past Fiona and Morgan and came to rest on the crystals and gemstones in the case. Her eyes widened slightly as she noticed the crystal nearest Fiona pulsing with vibrant color. "Ah, you are interested in the crystals."

"Just one gemstone, actually." Fiona pointed at the largest one. Its color pulsed rapidly from purple to red to brown.

"The alexandrite." The woman glided behind the length of the case and came to a stop opposite them. She slid the door in the back of the case open and with long, blue-glittered fingernails she plucked the stone out. She laid it on a black velvet pillow and pushed it across the top of the case towards them. "Alexandrite is a stone of prosperity and longevity. It balances the mind and emotions and pacifies the soul. It promotes spiritual growth. The owners of this stone may be surprised at what it adds to their lives."

Fiona cocked a brow at the woman. "Surprised? What do you mean?"

Cassiopeia shrugged. "Just that it will add interesting depth and dimension. It's a beauty, isn't it?"

"It certainly is." Fiona picked up the stone and angled it this way and that, watching it glow with a kaleidoscope of purple and red hues.

"This one has an extraordinary cut. See how it reflects a rainbow of colors depending on how you hold it to the light?" Cassiopeia asked.

"Emerald by day and ruby by night," Fiona quoted from the cryptic note that had sent the sisters on their quest. She walked to the window, angling the alexandrite into the sunlight. The stone glowed with a palette of blues and greens.

"Amazing, isn't it?" Cassiopeia looked at Fiona knowingly. "It reflects different colors in natural light than it does in incandescent light."

Fiona walked back and handed it to Morgan, who placed the stone in her palm then held it up to eye level. "It's fascinating. How did you come by it?" Fiona asked.

"That particular stone comes from a unique collection. A renowned gemologist from Salem, Massachusetts, recently passed and her estate sold off most of the collection. I was lucky enough to procure it." Cassiopeia spread her hands to indicate the contents of the case.

"Would you happen to know the person's name?" Fiona asked.

"Of course. It was Amity Jones. Have you heard of her?"

Morgan and Fiona exchanged a look. They hadn't heard of her, but it was obvious the stone was the one they were looking for.

"No, but we'll take the stone." Fiona nestled the gemstone back onto the black velvet pillow. She glanced into the case at its price tag of one hundred dollars. "Would you let it go for ninety?"

Cassiopeia smiled a warm smile that crinkled the corners of her eyes slightly. "I suppose I could let it go for that. I can see it's going to a good home."

"That it is." Fiona pulled a wad of cash out of her pocket.

Cassiopeia rang up the purchase then put the stone into a velvet covered jewelry box which she slid into a metallic fabric drawstring-bag. She handed the bag to Fiona. "I hope to see you again soon," she called after them as they exited to the street.

***

As Fiona and Morgan left the shop, a dark-haired man in a black leather jacket came from behind the black curtain. He joined Cassiopeia at the window where she watched the sisters walking down the street. The man was no stranger to the Blackmoore sisters. In fact, he'd been watching out for them for years now, helping them and guiding them, though the sisters would never know how much. His job of keeping them safe and out of trouble was not an easy one and he took it seriously.

"Their powers are getting stronger, but they are still not fully developed." Cassiopeia turned concerned eyes on Mateo. "Do you think they're ready?"

Mateo's handsome face creased with worry. His velvety brown eyes remained on the two sisters until they disappeared out of sight. "They will have to be ready."

Cassiopeia sighed and turned away from the window. "I don't know why we have to use all the subterfuge. You could have just given them the stone."

Mateo shook his head. "It's what was written by the ancient energy masters. They needed to seek it out for themselves."

Cassiopeia waved her hand. "I suppose. Sometimes those ancient energy masters and their mystifying rules can be so tedious. I'm just glad to get rid of the darn thing, I didn't like the idea of having it here in the shop where any old paranormal could come in and take notice of it."

Cassiopeia had purchased the crystals from Amity Jones for more than just shop inventory. They needed a safe place for the keystone, one where Fiona would be likely to find it, but also where they could keep it away from their enemies. Cassiopeia could easily have hidden the stone if she sensed an enemy paranormal about to enter the shop. And since the items which were purchased from the estate, as well as the names of those who purchased them, were kept private, no one who knew Amity Jones had possessed the special stone would be able to find out where it had gone.

The paranormal guild had hoped they could rely on Morgan's intuition to bring the girls to the shop. That had proven true today.

"Luckily, you didn't have to keep it for long. I knew my girls would come through." Mateo pulled out a black motorcycle helmet from under the counter.

Cassiopeia clutched at his arm as he turned to leave. "Remember, your role is to guide only."

"I remember." His eyes drifted out the window again. "But they may need some help and I intend to be there when they do."

"They'll have all the help they need if they learn to accept the spells. The spells will make them more powerful."

"Right. But they're stubborn. It's taken a long time for them to accept the powers they have." Mateo grimaced. "I don't know if they'll readily accept using spells."

"They'll have to if they want to get the relic back."

"Maybe. Maybe they can get it back with just the powers they have."

Cassiopeia cast a doubtful glance back out the window even though Morgan and Fiona were now well out of sight. "I'm not sure about those two. What about the younger one, Jolene? I heard she is much stronger."

"She is the most powerful and the one that is coming along the fastest with her gifts."

Cassiopeia turned a quizzical eye on Mateo. "Do I detect a hint of something more than professional interest? You know that can never happen. The bloodlines can't mingle—at least not

without some powerful ... and dangerous ... magic.
"

Mateo arched a brow and flashed the handsome smile that even after all these years still caught Cassiopeia off guard.

He kissed the top of her head, put the helmet on and started toward the door. "Never say never, sweetheart. Never say never."

**

The sun slanted through the windshield of Fiona's large black pickup truck, heating the inside to sweltering. Morgan and Fiona slid in and Fiona blasted the air conditioning then cracked the windows to let the hot air out. Fiona fanned herself with her hand as she watched the tourists walk under the colorful striped canopies that shaded the old storefronts along the brick-paved sidewalk.

The smell of fried seafood made her stomach grumble. A little boy trotted by with an ice cream cone clutched in his right hand while his left hand was firmly clasped in that of his mother. His short legs worked overtime to keep up with his parent as the mound of ice cream wobbled precariously on top of the cone.

Fiona licked her lips, thinking an ice cream would taste pretty good right now. It was just about lunchtime, too. Maybe she would have ice cream for lunch if Morgan didn't insist on heading home too quickly. A rustling sound from the seat beside her brought her attention back to the matter at hand.

Morgan lifted the velvet covered box out of the bag, snapped it open and retrieved the stone. She placed it in the palm of her hand. "Darn thing doesn't glow like it does when *you* hold it. Do you really think this is the stone in the note?"

"Yes. It makes perfect sense now. I know we were looking for a stone shaped like a key but have you ever seen a gemstone in that shape?" Fiona asked.

Morgan shook her head.

"Me, either. It would be incredibly difficult to cut one shaped like an actual key, so this must be it. And your intuition did lead us here..." Fiona let her voice trail off.

Fiona, Morgan and their two sisters, Celeste and Jolene, each had special paranormal gifts. Fiona's gift had to do with crystals and gemstones. Her energy meshed with the energy inside them and made them more powerful. She was able to amplify the mystical properties of them and had recently started to hone that gift to be able to use them for other purposes, like defending themselves against other paranormals.

Morgan's gift was intuition. The eldest Blackmoore sister had once told Fiona that she always thought she was just a little more observant than the average person. Turns out it was a true gift, and that gift had led them to this very store one hour away from their seaside home in Noquitt, Maine.

They'd been searching for the stone in various shops and estate sales for months when Morgan had suddenly gotten the urge to come here. Good thing they'd followed up on it, since it appeared that the stone had been waiting for them here the whole time.

Fiona knew it had to be the stone they were looking for by the way it practically pulled them into the shop. As soon as Fiona had parked the car here, Morgan had honed in on the *Eye of Newt* like a dowsing rod finding an underground spring.

It was about time they found the darn thing. She knew its discovery meant they would have to embark on a mission to find the relic. The stone was just the first part of that, according to the note.

This past winter they'd spent a week in a remote part of Costa Rica on a false lead that Dorian Hall, the head of the paranormal agency, had given them over Thanksgiving. When that didn't pan out, the trail went cold. Then this note surfaced. Fiona was glad the trail was closer to home.

They were paid handsomely for these adventures, but the girls didn't do it for the money. They did it to make sure the ancient relics stayed away from those who would use them for evil. Like Dr. Bly who had held their mother hostage for seven years, draining her of her paranormal abilities and nearly killing her in the process. Fiona and her sisters would work for free if it meant keeping these important relics from *him*, but there was no sense telling Dorian that. If she wanted to pay them for it, that just sweetened the pot.

"At least now the message makes a little more sense," Morgan said.

Fiona recited the message from heart: "*The key stone that is emerald by day and ruby by night will unlock the path to viewing the future - at the source of the stone you will find the first clue.*"

"I wondered how a stone could be emerald during the day and ruby at night. I hadn't considered alexandrite," Fiona admitted.

Morgan frowned down at the stone. "How does it do that?"

"It's in the way the minerals absorb the light," Fiona explained as she eyed the ice cream shop down the street. "Different types of light cause it to reflect differently and your eye sees a different color."

"So what do you think *'at the source of the stone you will find the first clue'* means?"

"That's why I asked where she got the stone. I assume that's the source."

"Or the store we just bought it from could be the source."

"Or where the stone was originally mined from could be the source." Fiona studied Morgan. "But what does your gut instinct tell you?"

"It tells me it has something to do with this Amity Jones person. I felt it as soon as she said the name. But I also feel like we could be walking into a heap load of trouble."

Fiona's attention was on a pair of middle-aged women coming out of the ice cream shop holding double dip cones. "When aren't we walking into a heap load of trouble?"

"True, and at least we have a lot of practice fighting off the bad guys, so trouble isn't that big of a problem anymore."

"Right, as long as we keep our skills honed ... and watch out for Celeste."

Worry over Celeste stole Fiona's attention from the ice cream. She feared for her sister whenever they came up against a paranormal enemy. Celeste's gift was seeing ghosts.

Unfortunately, that didn't help defend her against paranormal attacks. Sure, she was a top-notch karate expert, but she wasn't able to singe people with hot rocks like Fiona, or zap them with streams of energy like Jolene or even use her intuition to anticipate their next move like Morgan. Sometimes the opponent's spirit could help her out by pointing out weak spots, but that was only if the spirit appeared—which didn't always happen. For the most part, she was defenseless.

"But at least we have Jolene. She makes up for it."

"And you've got some pretty good skills with your rocks now," Morgan added.

Fiona had recently perfected the skill of turning small stones into blazing hot projectiles that she could fling at an enemy, inflicting them with hot, searing pain, which usually made them turn and run. It had come in handy quite a few times, already.

"So what do we do now?" Fiona wanted to tap Morgan's intuition as to how to proceed. She hoped would include a single serving chocolate chip with jimmies in a waffle cone. "It says to follow the source, but the source—Amity Jones—is dead."

"That's a good question. I think we need to find out what this Amity Jones was up to. Maybe we can figure out if she was working with someone and question them."

Fiona watched a motorcycle whiz by, the sunlight glinting off the rider's black helmet. She shut the truck off and opened her door. "Good thinking, and I know just the person who can figure that out ... after we get an ice cream."

Chapter 2

It took a little over an hour to get from Freeport to the girls' home town of Noquitt, Maine. Fiona always loved the feeling of pulling up to their giant seaside mansion, a palatial home that had been built three hundred years ago by one of their ancestors. The house which stood three stories high sat on a picturesque point of land that bordered the Atlantic Ocean on one side and a channel leading to the quaint Perkins Cove on the other.

The sweet smell of baking drew them from the oak foyer down the hall and into the black and white tiled kitchen. It warmed her heart to see her mother, Johanna Blackmoore, removing a tray of golden brown cookies from the oven. A little over a year ago, Johanna had been so ill that she'd been reduced to a shadow of her former self, unable to get around without the aid of a wheelchair. Seeing her standing in the kitchen making cookies assured Fiona that her mother was, indeed, recovering nicely.

"*Meow.*" Belladonna, the family cat trotted out to greet them. Her luxurious white fur looked freshly groomed. She sniffed the hem of Morgan's jeans, then the heel of Fiona's sandal before peering up at them disdainfully with her ice blue eyes. She flicked her tail and trotted off into the sitting room.

"What's with her?" Morgan asked.

Johanna shrugged. "Probably mad you didn't bring her something."

"Did you bring *me* something?" Their youngest sister, Jolene, poked her head in from the sitting room. Her wavy brunette hair was tied back in a ponytail. Her ice blue eyes—a Blackmoore family trait and, therefore, exact replicas of Morgan, Fiona and Celeste's—sparkled with excitement.

They'd called ahead to tell her about finding the keystone and to arrange a family meeting. Jolene was a whiz with the computer and it fell on her to do any computer research associated with the girls' extracurricular paranormal exploits. If there was a lead to be followed up concerning Amity Jones, Jolene would find it.

"No, we didn't bring you anything. We went straight to the shop, picked up the crystal and headed straight home," Fiona said.

Jolene leaned against the doorjamb, her arms folded across her chest. "Really? Then what's that on your shirt?" Jolene squinted at an area near Fiona's stomach.

Fiona looked down to see a brown stain marring her lavender cotton tee shirt. "Jimmies, I guess."

Jolene looked incredulous. "You had ice cream and didn't bring me any?"

"It would have melted."

"Uh-huh. I'm gonna remember that." Jolene pushed off from the doorjamb and returned to the sitting room. "Come on in here. I've looked up Amity Jones. It seems she was quite a big collector of crystals and rocks."

"Did you find anything to indicate that she might be someone who would have an ancient energy infused relic?" Morgan asked.

"There are some rumors that she had mystical powers and she did live in Salem, Mass."

Johanna appeared in the doorway, balancing her cane in one hand and a plate of cookies in the other. "Salem has long been thought to be a center of paranormal activity."

"That's right. People mistook paranormal activity for witchcraft." Morgan shot her mother a warning look.

Johanna knew she wasn't supposed to be tottering around without the full use of her cane. Fiona took the tray of cookies and helped Johanna to the white linen slip-covered couch despite her mother's efforts to shoo her away.

"We all know there's no such thing as witches," Celeste called out from the hallway shortly before appearing in the doorway, her short-cropped, blonde hair spiked up as if she'd been running her hands through it … or standing on her head which Fiona figured was more likely, considering her sister's love of yoga.

"We do?" Johanna asked. "How do we know that?"

Morgan laughed. "Well, our gifts are out of the ordinary, but we don't use spells or charms or even ride on broomsticks."

"*We* don't," Johanna said. "But maybe other people do. Who's to say others don't have unique gifts that are similar to the traditional ones that people associate with witches?"

Fiona frowned. "Have you ever seen anyone actually cast a spell or ride a broomstick?"

"Or turn someone into a bat?" Jolene added.

"No."

"But you've seen plenty of people with paranormal powers," Fiona said. "People that can see ghosts, like Celeste. People that can bend energy like Jolene or enhance crystals like I can, or that have a way with herbs and uncanny intuition like Morgan. I think what really happened back then is that people didn't understand paranormal abilities, and they persecuted those who had them."

21

"Or people that didn't even have paranormal abilities were persecuted because someone either didn't like them or wanted them out of the way. But that's not really our concern right now. Right now, we need to figure out what, exactly, this 'key' stone is trying to tell us and where we should go to find out," Jolene said. "Speaking of which, let's see this thing."

Fiona removed the stone from its box and held it out for them all to look at. Under the interior lighting it glowed red and purple. She crossed to the window with its panoramic view of the ocean and held the stone up, watching it change to green and blue.

"That's beautiful," Jolene said.

"Did Luke say any more about exactly what it is we're looking for?" Celeste asked Morgan. Luke was Morgan's boyfriend and worked for Dorian Hall.

Morgan shook her head.

"What about Dorian Hall?" Jolene leaned over to look toward the kitchen. Dorian had been known to suddenly appear mysteriously at their front door. No one would be surprised if she walked in right now with further instructions. Actually, it would be nice if she did. They could use another lead.

"She didn't say anything more. Just what was in the note, and that she heard Dr. Bly was after the relic and it was extremely important that we find it." Morgan got up from the overstuffed chair, dumping Belladonna on the floor making the cat let out a wail of disapproval before trotting over to Johanna and jumping into her lap.

"Dorian thinks everything she wants is extremely important," Fiona said.

"It usually is," Celeste pointed out.

"Especially when it has to do with Bly," Johanna chimed in.

"*Meyess!*" Belladonna added.

Morgan reached around Jolene and opened the desk drawer. She pulled out the cryptic note and placed it on the surface of the desk. They all leaned forward to look at the paper. Even Belladonna roused herself from Johanna's lap and leapt silently onto the desk, pushing at the paper with her paw, setting it off-kilter.

Jolene straightened the paper.

Belladonna pushed it again.

Jolene slid the paper away from the cat and read the note aloud, *"The key stone that is emerald by day and ruby by night will unlock the path to viewing the future - at the source of the stone you will find the first clue."*

"We know the key stone that is ruby at night and emerald during the day is the alexandrite gemstone you have in your hand," Morgan said to Fiona.

"Right. So what do you think it means by 'will unlock the path to viewing the future'?" Fiona asked.

Morgan shrugged. "Must be the path to finding the relic I guess."

"At the source of the stone you'll find the first clue." Jolene pressed her lips together. "That is the part that's confusing. How do we know where the source of the stone is?"

"I think our best bet for that is the collector," Morgan said. "Amity Jones."

"But she's dead," Jolene said. "What about this shop in Freeport where you got the stone?"

Morgan shook her head. "My gut instinct is that we need to follow the trail from Amity Jones. I did get kind of a strange vibe from the shop owner, Cassiopeia, but I don't think that is where we need to look."

Jolene sat at the desk and opened the laptop. "I've taken the liberty of researching into this Amity Jones. She died a few months ago. Her next of kin is a niece who has been handling the estate, a Nancy Baumann."

"Maybe she knows something?" Celeste suggested.

"Or maybe there are other items in the estate that might be clues. I say we go out there and see what we can find out," Fiona said.

"*Meow*!" Belladonna nodded her head.

Morgan checked her watch. "That sounds like a good idea. If we leave now, we can be settled at a hotel just before dinner. Maybe we can make an appointment to go out to the house. Between Jolene's insight into auras and energy, and my intuition, we might pick up on something."

"Maybe we'll luck out and Amity's ghost will show up and tell us exactly what we need to know," Celeste said.

"Sounds good." Fiona turned to Johanna. "You'll be okay here at home alone?"

Johanna made a face. "Of course. I stayed here alone plenty of times before you girls were born. I'm not an old lady who needs constant care, you know."

"*Merow*!" Belladonna looked up at them expectantly.

"I don't think *she* will be okay staying at home, though," Johanna added, nodding toward the cat.

"Good point." Morgan said. "We'd better find a hotel that takes cats. You know how Belladonna can be when we leave her behind."

Fiona scowled at the cat. "I sure do. The last time we left her behind, I came home to find my charm bracelet on the floor and my favorite goldfish charm missing."

"She loves to play with shiny things. She probably batted the charms around. Did you check in the cracks of the old floor boards and under your bureau?" Celeste asked.

Fiona looked at the cat that looked back innocently. "I looked everywhere and couldn't find it."

"Well, it must be somewhere," Morgan said. "It didn't just disappear."

"No, I'm sure it didn't." Fiona narrowed her eyes at Belladonna. "I'm pretty sure she ate it."

Belladonna narrowed her eyes at Fiona then let out a not-so-innocent belch, "*Murp.*" She hopped off the desk and trotted out of the room.

Chapter 3

Salem, Massachusetts, a beautiful seaside town, filled with old colonial homes and steeped in history, was the site of the infamous witch trials of 1692, but the town had been around a lot longer than that. Located on the North Shore of Massachusetts, its position at the mouth of a natural bay made it one of the most important seaports in early America.

The girls had scoured the internet and found a comfortable hotel in a historic brick home with a view of the Salem waterfront, which was at the end of the street. They booked a suite at Craig's Hotel, one with a common area, kitchenette and adjoining rooms, as was the custom when they were out on a job.

Jolene was glad when Morgan finally stopped their SUV in front of the hotel, so she would no longer have to listen to the constant whining coming from the cat carrier.

"Sorry, Buddy, we have to keep you in this crate. You know how hotel people are." Celeste rubbed Belladonna's forehead through the mesh webbing at the front of the canvas cat carrier.

"Merough!"

"Yes, it is tough, but they do expect you to be in a carrier and crated in the room. If they know you are going to be running about willy-nilly, they'll never rent to us."

"*Murpp.*"

"It won't be that long."

Morgan twisted in the driver's seat to peer in the carrier. "Perhaps we should actually keep her confined to the crate like we promised the hotel owner. Though I doubt *that* would keep her from getting into trouble."

Belladonna had a way of turning up in the strangest places. The sisters didn't know how it happened. The places she appeared were usually too far for her to get to on her own. It was simply one of the many mysterious things the girls had come to accept as normal when it came to their cat.

"Let's get settled." Jolene hopped out of the SUV and popped the tailgate open. The sound of a motorcycle whizzing by caught her attention. "Hey, is that Mateo?"

It was impossible to tell. The motorcycle was now too far away and the driver had a helmet on. But what Jolene *could* tell was that there was a slim woman on the back, her long dark hair flying out from beneath her helmet. Mateo with a woman? Jolene turned around to find Morgan smirking at her.

"Jealous?" Morgan teased.

"No." Jolene's cheeks heated as something sharp stabbed her heart. Indigestion? Certainly not jealousy. She didn't have anything going on with Mateo ... well, except for that electrifying kiss they'd shared on Thanksgiving. *And* those fluttery feelings she always had when he was around.

Mateo was a nomad who came and went like the wind. Even though he always seemed to show up when she needed him most, he wasn't reliable boyfriend material. Not that Jolene was even in the market for a boyfriend. She preferred to be on her own. She hefted her overnight bag onto her shoulder, picked up the cat carrier and proceeded into the hotel.

The lobby was decorated in pale yellow with white trim. Antique paintings in gold frames lined the walls. A welcoming fire burned in the marble-surrounded fireplace despite the fact that it was almost the end of June and quite warm out. Antique furniture sat atop jewel-toned oriental rugs. The desk was made from quarter-sawn oak, polished to a honey gold shine.

A middle-aged man, plump around the waist and wearing black-rimmed glasses, smiled as Jolene approached.

"Hi. We reserved a suite. Blackmoore."

"*Meow.*"

His smile faded as his gaze drifted from Jolene's face to the cat carrier. "Right. The people with the cat." He looked over her shoulder as Morgan, Celeste and Fiona entered the lobby. "Do you have a proper crate? We require the cat be kept in a crate if you're out, with their cat box."

"Yes," Jolene assured him. "It's all in the car. We'll bring it up once we get settled."

"Harrumph. Very well, then." He typed on the computer then dug under the desk and came out with two cards. "We only give out two keys."

"That's fine. We usually go everywhere together anyway." Jolene grabbed the keys and turned away from the desk.

"Top of the stairs and to the right," the man called after her.

Their rooms were decorated with antiques, similar to the lobby, with four-poster beds and fireplaces in every room. Comfortable antique reproduction furniture was in the common area. A small kitchenette took up one corner of the room and there was a small table where Jolene set up her laptop. The room was quaint, with wide floorboards that creaked when they walked on them. There was a slightly musty smell of old books wafting out from the many book shelves that were in every nook and cranny. It was air-conditioned, but stuffy.

Morgan opened a window to let some air in. A soft, lulling swish of traffic filled the room along with the faint smell of the sea.

"I'm starving," Fiona said.

Jolene's stomach growled. "It *is* supper time."

"We can get something after we call Nancy Baumann." Morgan made the call and put her cellphone on speaker, the sound of ringing filling the room.

"Hello?"

"Hi, Nancy? My name is Morgan Blackmoore. I recently bought some crystals and gemstones that came from your aunt's estate. I was wondering if she had any more that you hadn't yet sold off?"

"You mean those rocks? No, I didn't find any others in her belongings."

Morgan's shoulders sagged with disappointment. "Do you still have a lot of her stuff left? My sisters and I are avid collectors and would like to know more about the rocks. Especially if she kept records on how she obtained them ..."

"Records? Yes, she had journals and whatnot. Should I have saved them? They were just old scribblings, so I tossed them."

"You threw them out?"

"Couple of months ago. All that's left now in the house is some furniture and kitchenware. Are you interested in any of that?"

"Maybe. We were mostly interested in the rocks, though. Or anything that has to do with them." Morgan would use any excuse to get into the house. The sisters never knew when they might pick up an energy trail or run into a helpful ghost.

"Well, there are a few old boxes in the attic. I don't know what's in there, but I can get those down if you'd like to look at them."

Morgan raised her brows at her sisters, who all nodded enthusiastically. "We would love that."

"Okay. Well, I'm not going back over tonight. What do you say we meet tomorrow around ten?"

"Sounds perfect." Morgan wrote down the address the woman provided then snapped the phone shut.

"Well, it's disappointing that she didn't keep those journals and doesn't have any other stones, but maybe we'll see something at her house that helps us out," Celeste said.

"Maybe there's something in those boxes," Jolene suggested.

"It would be helpful if we knew what we were looking for," Fiona added.

"*Mew!*" Belladonna hopped up onto the windowsill and blinked out the window.

Scratch, scratch. Clank.

"Is something outside the window?" Morgan's face turned serious.

Jolene knew what that meant: Morgan's intuition was kicking in. Jolene bolted to the window and ripped the curtain aside. No one was there.

"Nothing?" Morgan asked.

Jolene pushed up the window and leaned out to look down. They were on the second floor. A black wrought iron fire escape wound its way up the building beside the window. Below, was a narrow alley with an opening at each end. "Maybe someone was cutting through the alley."

"It sounded like it was right here on the fire escape," Celeste said.

"*Merow!*"

Jolene pulled her head in and stood back to let her sister look out. "There's nothing down there. Just an old broom. Maybe it was on the fire escape and fell down."

Morgan grimaced. "Maybe."

Jolene didn't think her sister looked convinced.

Fiona said dismissively, "I think you guys are being paranoid. Who would be spying on us?

No one even knows we're here, besides Luke, Jake and Cal," Fiona rattled off their boyfriends' names.

"Well, there is one other person," Morgan said.

"Who?"

"That woman from *Eye of Newt*. We asked where she got the crystals and stones from so maybe she put two and two together and figured we would come here."

"But why would she follow us? She could come here herself. She already knew the stone was from Amity Jones' estate."

Morgan shrugged. "I have no idea why she would follow us, but if it's not her then who else knows we're here and why would they be lurking outside our window?"

Chapter 4

They ate breakfast in their kitchenette. They'd brought a few things from home, like coffee, milk, cereals, and Celeste's healthy flaxseed, cottage cheese and wheatgrass juice. They didn't linger over their coffees because they'd gotten up late and they had an appointment to keep.

On the way to the SUV, they passed the hotel owner. He was using the broom they'd seen laying in the alley the night before to sweep dirt out of the lobby onto the street. "You girls have a nice day. I hope you've got that cat of yours crated up there."

"Yes, of course. We don't leave her out." Morgan crossed her fingers behind her back. They always instructed the hotel staff they didn't want housekeeping and left Belladonna out to do as she pleased. If they didn't, she'd just escape anyway and besides, they knew she would never do any damage.

The man glanced up towards their room. "I thought I saw her in the window."

"No, must've been just a shadow."

He nodded, watching them under hooded eyes as they walked to their SUV.

Jolene got the GPS map working on her smartphone so she directed Morgan west, through the town, toward Amity Jones' house. As they meandered through the streets, Jolene pointed out various museums, houses and restaurants, all seemingly set up to cater to the witch-seeking tourist trade. "Boy, this place really is into the witchcraft."

"Tourist trap. Every business is trying to capitalize on the history of the town." Fiona's head turned as they drove by something that caught her eye. "Though I wouldn't mind trying out the Toil and Trouble Ice Cream Parlor."

"You do owe me an ice cream," Jolene reminded her sister.

Morgan followed the GPS map and turned onto a side street that headed away from the center of town. Fifteen minutes later they found themselves on an isolated road flanked by thick forest on either side. Giant oak trees lined the road, their leaves creating a canopy overhead which shaded the car from the heat of the day.

The late Amity Jones' house was actually a small cottage. Faded dark brown shakes decorated the exterior. The paint peeled and bubbled on the white trim. A shutter hung cockeyed from a front window. The lawn was overgrown.

It might have given Celeste the creeps if it wasn't for the sunlight filtering through the trees in happy dancing dots and the birds chirping cheerily. An old Volvo sat parked in the driveway. When they pulled up behind it, she said, "Looks like she's here."

The sisters picked their way through the weeds up the path and onto the porch. The front door was open. A screen door, the mesh torn and drooping down in one corner, was the only thing barring entry.

Morgan tapped her fist on the screen door's frame. "Nancy? It's me, Morgan Blackmoore. We talked on the phone. I brought my three sisters."

Silence.

Morgan knocked louder. "Nancy?"

"Should we just go in?" Jolene nodded at the open door. "Maybe she's in the attic and left the door open so we could just come in."

The hinges squeaked as Morgan slowly open the screen door. They saw that the inside of the cottage wasn't in much better shape than the outside. Wallpaper peeled down from the water-stained ceiling in a few spots. Squares of worn, wooden flooring peeked out from a layer of dust indicating where furniture once stood. "Nancy! We're here!" Morgan yelled so as to alert Nancy that someone else was in the house.

Celeste knew Morgan didn't like just walking into someone's home and neither did she. She looked around in the corners hoping Amity's ghost would appear, but was left disappointed when she didn't see even a hint of swirling mist. She pushed down feelings of inadequacy.

Though she knew that the information she got from ghosts had been instrumental in helping them in other cases, she still felt like she didn't pull her weight—especially when it came to altercations with opposing paranormals. Her karate expertise allowed her to kick butt with regular people, but no matter how powerful or well placed a karate kick was no match for a paranormal evildoer with an energy gun.

She hated having to depend on her sisters to fight off the bad guys. The least she could do was make up for it by playing a bigger role in gathering information. But she couldn't do that if ghosts refused to show up.

Unlike Morgan, Jolene had no qualms about wandering around and opening the drawers of the few pieces of furniture that were left. She turned to Celeste. "What do you think? Will we see Amity's ghost?"

Celeste's spirits sunk even lower. "I've dialed up my senses but I don't think there are any ghosts here."

The girls normally shut down the senses that allowed them to make full use of their gifts. It was too much of a drain to be always 'on' when it came to energy sensitivity. They only dialed up their powers on certain occasions.

"There are a lot of energy streams here," Jolene said. "Maybe one of them will tell me something."

"Nancy!" Morgan's voice was tinged with worry. "Nancy isn't answering, but her car is here. I don't have a good feeling about this."

Jolene stopped her snooping in the doorway to the next room. She said in a small voice, "I don't think Nancy is going to answer."

Celeste, Fiona and Morgan ran to Jolene's side. The doorway was to a kitchen that hadn't been updated since the 1950s. The counters were white and gold speckled laminate edged with a strip of aluminum. The pine cupboard doors and drawers hung open. The utensils, plates, cups and saucers that had presumably occupied the cupboards and drawers sat piled on a rickety kitchen table.

But Jolene wasn't looking at any of that. Her eyes were trained on the green and black tiled floor where a lifeless woman was on her back with a letter opener stuck in her chest.

Chapter 5

"No!" Fiona raced to the body, knelt down and felt for a pulse. Nothing. Fiona's hand went instinctively to the carnelian stones she kept in her pocket. The stones had proven to have immense powers of healing at other times. But it was too late. The woman was already gone and the healing stones weren't powerful enough to bring someone back from the dead.

"She's dead?" Celeste's eyes drifted sadly from Fiona to the body.

Fiona nodded. She saw Celeste's eyes dart around the room as if looking for something. Fiona realized her sister was looking for the ghost of the woman on the floor. Sometimes ghosts appeared at the time of death, but usually Celeste didn't see them until much later. "Any sign of her?"

"No." Celeste shook her head.

"That's too bad." Morgan pointed at the wound that had to have happened face to face. "Her ghost could tell us who killed her."

"And why," Jolene added.

"Maybe this is why." Morgan knelt down, gently opened the dead woman's hand, and plucked something small out of it. She held it for the others to see.

It was a torn scrap of paper with black markings on it.

"She was holding something in her hand when she was killed." Celeste stated the obvious.

"Something that the killer grabbed." Jolene looked over the piece of paper. "He must not have realized that he left this scrap behind. What do you think it's from?"

"I don't know, but I think it's important enough for us to keep, and that we'd better call the police," Morgan said.

Jolene sighed. "Maybe we should look around a little bit first." She glanced down at the body ruefully. "I mean, I know a woman is dead, but this will probably be our only chance to look for clues to the relic that might be inside this house."

"Seems like the killer probably took the clue." Celeste pointed to the scrap of paper that Jolene was putting carefully into her front pocket.

"Maybe there are more clues." Fiona glanced around. The house was nearly empty with just a few sticks of furniture. What could possibly be still here?

Morgan narrowed her eyes. "Maybe." She gnawed on her bottom lip.

Fiona knew her sister was dialing up her senses, heightening the power of her gift of intuition. Maybe she would be able to get a sense of what happened. Fiona could see Jolene doing the same, probably searching the house for energy patterns. Fiona looked at Celeste and shrugged. Neither of them had the types of gifts that would give them insight into what had happened here or what Amity Jones knew about the relic.

Jolene's eyes raked over the body, following a path from the body to the front door. "There's some kind of unusual energy trail. It has a distinctive marker. A yellow and red pattern."

"From the killer. Was she killed by a paranormal?" Fiona asked.

"I'm not sure," Jolene said.

They looked at the body. The poor woman didn't appear to have been killed using paranormal methods. In fact, the letter opener sticking out of her chest seemed to indicate she'd been killed in a very old-fashioned way.

The sisters quickly poked around the house, opening drawers, looking in all the rooms. Jolene even went up to the attic where she found two boxes, but neither one contained anything helpful. There was nothing in the house that gave them even the slightest clue as to what kind of relic they were looking for.

"We'd better call the cops now," Celeste said. "Someone might have seen us drive out here, and we don't want someone telling the cops we were here for hours before calling them."

Morgan made the 911 call then they went out to wait on the front steps.

It didn't take long for three police cars to pull up. A tall, thin man got out of one of them. His tired eyes in his haggard face regarded them with suspicion. "I'm Detective Peterson. Who's the person who called this in?"

"I am," Morgan answered.

"And you say there's a body in there? How do you know?" He eyed warily the cottage's open front door.

"We had an appointment with a Nancy Bauman." Morgan nodded at the door. "The door was open, just as you see it now, and we thought we were meant to go in. We found a woman's body in the kitchen, and we're guessing it's her."

Detective Peterson gestured for the cops and crime scene crew to go in. As they streamed past the girls, Peterson asked, "And just how do you know she was murdered?"

Morgan winced. "It's pretty obvious when you see the body."

"And since you were in there, I suppose your fingerprints will be all over the place." His eyes narrowed. "You young ladies don't seem too upset at finding a dead body. Just what is your business here?"

Fiona answered, trying not to sound defensive, "We had an appointment to look at some of Nancy's late aunt's things. We bought some crystals that belonged to her estate, earlier this week."

Jolene added helpfully, "The woman who lived here was a famous crystal and gemstone collector, Amity Jones. Her niece, who we assume is the one in there, was handling the estate."

Peterson waved a hand impatiently. "Yes, yes, I know all about that. You girls stay out here." His eyes narrowed again. And don't leave." He pushed past them up the steps muttering, "I hope you didn't mess up the crime scene."

"Well, we might as well look around out here while they're doing their thing inside," Jolene announced as she jumped up eagerly.

"Look for what?" Fiona asked in surprise.

Jolene shrugged. "Evidence? I don't know why Nancy was killed, but if it had something to do with our gemstone then the killer might be a person of interest to us. Best we know as much as we can."

They spread out over the front yard.

Fiona looked for physical evidence since her gifts didn't run toward having any kind of insight into the paranormal. Celeste looked for signs of an otherworldly presence. Morgan used her intuition to try to get a line on the killer. Jolene checked out energy patterns.

Jolene pointed toward the front path. "The same paranormal trail is here. The killer came in through the front door."

"Does that mean Nancy knew the killer?" Morgan wondered aloud.

"Maybe the killer had an appointment like we did," Celeste offered.

Fiona raised a brow. "Someone else looking for whatever information Amity had on the relic?"

"Possibly." Morgan's eyes drifted to the house. "I do sense a lot of disturbance, but nothing that tells me anything definitive."

"I just wish I could help out by talking to one of the women's ghosts but nobody's coming through," Celeste said.

"Hey, what's that?" Jolene's eyes were focused on the overgrown woods that sat just at the edge of the front yard.

Fiona looked over to see ... a flapping, black cape?

In a flash, Jolene was off and running. Fiona followed, reaching into her pocket to assure herself that the stones she used as energy-infused weapons were there at the ready.

"Over there!" Morgan pointed to the left and the girls spun in that direction.

Meow!

They skidded to a stop in front of a large black cat with glowing amber eyes. It was a fluffy cat almost exactly like the one that had been in the *Eye of Newt* shop.

Fiona scanned the horizon. There was no other sign of movement. "I guess it was just this cat."

"I only saw a flash of black but I thought it looked like a cape. Must've been mistaken." Jolene scratched the cat behind his ears and was rewarded with a loud purr and a rub against her leg.

Morgan and Celeste joined them. "I hope she isn't a stray." Celeste rubbed her hands along the cat's ribs. "She's well fed and her fur looks well groomed, so it looks like she's well taken care of."

The cat shot out her front paw, whacking at a pair of orange fire newts nestled in the damp leaves. The newts scurried away and the cat followed, pouncing on them and then letting them escape again.

"I guess she's just out here playing in the woods," Fiona said. She turned back towards the house. They hadn't gone far, but she couldn't see much of the house because there were so many trees in the woods. "We'd better go back. Detective Peterson might be looking for us."

"Yeah. I don't want to give him any reason to be suspicious of us, especially if he guesses that Nancy had something in her hand. He's going to wonder where that is." Jolene patted her pocket.

Fiona grimaced. "They'll assume the killer took whatever was in her hand."

They cleared the woods to find Peterson standing before the house, his mouth pursed in a hard line. "I thought I told you young ladies not to leave."

"Sorry," Morgan said. "We saw someone in the woods and we thought maybe it was the killer so we gave chase."

Peterson's eyes darted over the woods. "That's funny. I don't remember deputizing you. I hope you don't think you're going to be working this case. In fact, the four of you are persons of interest in the murder of Nancy Bauman, so I suggest you refrain from doing any amateur sleuthing."

The screen door opened and two men with 'Coroner's Department' written on the backs of their jackets brought the body out on a gurney. Everyone watched silently as it was wheeled down the front path. A policeman on the porch unrolled yellow crime scene tape.

Peterson turned back to the sisters. "I'm going to need statements from you. We need a few more minutes to go through the house but after that, I'll see you over by my car ... and this time, don't leave the yard." He ambled off toward the house.

The girls looked at each other, all fellow persons of interest.

"Well, at least he didn't mention her hand," Jolene whispered.

"Right, and it makes sense that he would be suspicious of us. I don't think he knows that we took anything," Celeste added softly.

"That's good, but unfortunately we're no better off than we were this morning," Morgan said. "In fact we're worse off, because now we don't even have Nancy to talk to and we didn't learn anything new."

"You're wrong about that," Fiona said. "We did learn one thing new. Whoever killed Nancy is quite likely after the same thing we are and they won't hesitate to kill in order to get it."

Chapter 6

After leaving Amity Jones' house, the girls headed back to the hotel. They sat around the small table in the kitchenette sipping freshly made French Press coffees while discussing their next move.

"*Meerow. Hiss.*"

"What's the matter, Belladonna?" Morgan asked.

"She's probably mad that we didn't bring her with us," Fiona said.

"Sorry. We can't very well bring you visiting to a stranger's house," Morgan explained.

Belladonna ignored Morgan, deciding instead to take an interest in sniffing Celeste's hand. After a few sniffs, she glared up at her and hissed. Then she turned her back and trotted into Celeste's bedroom.

"I think she smells that black cat on you. She's probably mad at us." Jolene pulled the piece of paper out of her pocket and put it on the table in front of them.

"She'll get over it." Celeste looked back over her shoulder at the doorway of her room. "I just hope she doesn't show her displeasure by hacking up a hairball in my bed."

Jolene tapped her finger on the little piece of paper. It was about a half-inch long and triangular, with black lines on it. "So, what do you guys think this is?"

Morgan slid it toward her, twisting it around so she could look at it from different angles. "Well, it's printed, and the paper is kind of shiny. Is it from the packaging of something?"

"You mean like maybe the lines are from a barcode?" Fiona picked the paper up and rubbed it between her forefinger and thumb. "I don't know. That doesn't feel quite right. It's too thick."

"*Mew!*" Belladonna hopped on the table and sniffed at the piece of paper in Fiona's hand.

"Looks like she's done being mad." Jolene plucked the paper from between Fiona's fingers and studied it.

Celeste glanced back at her room again, her forehead creasing. "Or she's exacted her revenge already."

"*Merow.*" Belladonna hopped down from the table and sidled over to the bookcase, rubbing her cheek against the row of books. She snaked out her paw and knocked a book off the shelf.

"What the ..." Jolene frowned at Belladonna. "I guess she really didn't like smelling that other cat on us."

"*Merow!*" Belladonna shot Jolene a look, then knocked another book off the shelf.

The book thudded on the floor upside down. Fiona bent to pick it up, her eyes going straight to the white block with the black lines on the back of the book, the ISBN number barcode.

"Wait a minute!" Fiona took the paper from Jolene. "This isn't a barcode from packaging—it's the ISBN barcode from the back of a book!"

"Let me see." Jolene reached over and retrieved the paper. "It's not the full code, but maybe I can figure out what book it is."

Jolene proceeded to futzed around online, muttering something about an app, while Fiona and the others sipped their coffee.

Belladonna, content that she'd done her job well, curled up in Morgan's lap and promptly went to sleep.

After a while, Jolene got her cellphone out and used it to scan the piece of paper, then she tapped furiously on the keys of her laptop. "Yes! I've got it!" She swung the laptop around so they could look at the screen where a book cover was displayed:

Uses of Crystals and Crystal Balls.

"Crystal balls," Fiona said. "What would be so important about that book that the killer would take it?"

"Obviously, Amity was interested in crystal balls."

"You mean like the crystal balls that people look into to see the future?" Celeste turned to Fiona. "You're the crystal expert. Are crystal balls like that real?"

Fiona knew that crystals and gemstones had special powers, especially when she touched them. She'd seen it with her own eyes that carnelian gemstones could speed up healing. She'd seen obsidian protect her and her sisters from negative energy and she'd also seen geodes drain their energy. She knew crystals were very powerful, but she wasn't sure they had the power to see into the future.

Of course she'd heard of crystal balls, but she'd always thought they were a fantasy, like witches flying on broomsticks. "I don't know. I don't have any experience with it myself, but then again maybe I haven't been looking into the right kinds of crystals."

"Wait a minute." Jolene jumped up from her chair and retrieved the cryptic note that had sent them on the journey in the first place.

She read the note out loud: *"The key stone that is emerald by day and ruby by night will unlock the path to viewing the future - at the source of the stone you will find the first clue."* She pointed to the middle. "That's it. We're looking for a crystal ball—that's what it means by viewing the future—the relic is a crystal ball."

Fiona tilted her head to read the note even though she had it memorized. "And the keystone— the stone we got in Freeport—unlocks the path."

Morgan's brows tugged together. "But if that were true, I think that would imply that the actual crystal ball was in Amity's house."

"I don't think that's what it means," Jolene disagreed. "The alexandrite stone unlocks the path to the crystal ball and the first *clue* is at the source of the stone. The source of the stone was Amity's house and this book is the first clue."

"The first clue ... meaning there are more to follow," Celeste said.

"Sounds like it," Morgan replied. "But how do we get the next clue?"

"And how does the alexandrite stone figure in?" Fiona asked. "It didn't really unlock any path other than to lead us to Amity because she owned it." Fiona pulled the stone out of her pocket and it flashed orange. "I have to think it has more use than just leading us to Amity's house."

Morgan reached over and touched the stone. Her brows arched upward in what Fiona recognized as a flash of intuition. "Oh yes, it has much more to do with it. This stone is very important. We need to keep it safe."

"But how does the book tie into this?" Celeste asked.

Jolene was behind the computer typing furiously. She swung it around again to show them the screen. "You know what they say: there are no coincidences in life. The person who wrote this book is named Opal Mines. And Opal happens to have a shop right here in Salem."

Chapter 7

Opal Mines' store was located on a small side street in downtown Salem. Morgan followed her sisters down the sidewalk to the awning-covered storefront. She paused as they passed the display window with its variety of crystal balls winking in the sunlight and refracting a rainbow of colors. Was one of these crystal balls the one they were looking for?

Bells tinkled as Jolene opened the door and they entered the small patchouli-scented store. It was loaded with crystal balls on every shelf and table, and in every display case. Morgan watched the colors of the orbs pulse as Fiona walked past them.

The eyebrows of an old, red-headed woman sitting behind the counter rose slightly when she noticed the orbs' reaction. She pushed herself up, her gnarled fist pressed into the ivory handle of her cane. "Help you girls?"

Morgan spoke up, "Yes, as a matter of fact we're looking for Opal Mines."

"What for?"

"We're interested in crystal balls. Amity Jones sent us," Morgan stretched the truth.

The woman's eyes narrowed at the mention of Amity and Morgan's intuition warned her that she might have made a mistake in telling the little white lie. It was *sort of* true in a round-about way that Amity had sent them, but she could tell this woman was sharp enough to see through them. Best to stick as close as possible to the truth if they wanted her cooperation.

"Amity sent you to see me?"

"Well, she didn't exactly send us. We bought a gemstone from her estate." Morgan leaned toward Opal and lowered her voice, "We're *very* interested in gemstones and crystals. Anyway, we talked to Amity's niece who's handling the estate and she mentioned the book you wrote." Did poor Nancy having a scrap of the book cover in her hand count as mentioning it? Morgan didn't think it was necessary to mention that Nancy was dead.

"Yeah, so?"

"We got the impression you were working with Amity on something." Okay, maybe this was stretching the truth more than she should. It was more like she *hoped* Opal had been working with Amity, or at least knew if Amity had a clue about a crystal ball, which might be the relic they were after. Morgan gestured to indicate the clear, round crystal balls in a display case. "Maybe something that had to do with crystal balls."

Opal laughed. "You mean scrying balls. I am famous for them. I wrote the book on it, you know." She hobbled out from behind the counter, her cane tapping on the floor as she pushed past Morgan, stopping to look in at the crystal balls in the display case.

Morgan looked over the woman's shoulder and thought she saw one of the balls flash with images as Opal gazed into it, but when Morgan blinked, she realized it was just a reflection of the Blackmoore sisters.

Opal turned quickly to face them. "I'm still not sure what you ladies actually want."

Jolene, with her usual impatience, cut to the chase, "What was Amity Jones working on that had to do with scrying balls?"

Opal shrugged. "I wish I knew."

"She wasn't working with you?" Celeste asked.

Opal shook her head. "I knew Amity for years, of course, both being from Salem and interested in crystals and all. She was a good friend. I know she was onto something, but she wouldn't tell me what it was."

If Opal knew Amity was onto something, then maybe someone else knew, too, which made

Morgan wonder if Amity had died because of it. She hadn't heard any controversy about the woman's death so she'd assumed it was of natural causes, but what if it wasn't? "Was Amity ill?"

Opal frowned. "Amity? She was as fit as a fiddle. It was a big shock when she died suddenly of that heart attack."

The girls exchanged a look of silent understanding. Heart attack or paranormal murder? Skilled paranormals could easily kill someone and make it appear like a heart attack. Negative energy used in a certain way could stop the heart, and if they were careful to not leave burn marks, no one would know what had caused the attack. They already suspected a paranormal killed Nancy, so it was becoming very clear that a paranormal was after the relic. Maybe even more than one? Possibly even Opal?

Opal leaned back and studied them shrewdly. "Now, you ladies come clean. What are you up to? Obviously you're after the same thing Amity was."

"We're not really sure what Amity was up to, either, but we are interested. Was there anything in particular she talked about or any place she was interested in?"

Opal crossed her hands over the top of her cane and leaned on it, her wrinkled face turning thoughtful. "She was tight lipped. But the one place she kept talking about was the Rebecca Nurse house. Something about the witch trials."

"Rebecca Nurse?"

"Yes, she was hung for witchcraft back in 1692. Her house is a museum now. Amity made a few trips over there, kept talking about it." Opal shrugged. "I don't really know much more."

Morgan's intuition told her that Opal *did* know more, but she wasn't about to trust four strangers with it. Pressing her on the matter would only backfire. "Okay, thanks. If you think of anything, will you let us know? We're staying at the Craig Hotel. Name's Blackmoore."

Something flickered in Opal's eyes at the mention of their name. "Blackmoore. Right."

Morgan could feel Opal's eyes following them as they exited the store.

"Well, that didn't get us very far." Fiona paused in front of an ice cream store, her attention captured by the menu of fifty-one flavors.

"No, but we at least have another lead. We need to get to this Rebecca Nurse place and maybe it will lead us somewhere else." Celeste tugged her sister away from the menu.

"And what about Opal?" Jolene asked. "Do you think she's friend or foe? I got the impression she was holding back."

Morgan glanced back at the shop in time to see Opal quickly pull back from the window. "Opal Mines has more to do with this, I know it. Let's just hope she isn't the killer, because if she is, her sights might now be set on us."

Chapter 8

Jolene agreed with Morgan—Opal knew more than she was letting on. She'd tried to read the woman's aura, but everything had been fuzzy like a television station that wasn't tuned in. She didn't know if Opal was a skilled paranormal and blocking her aura reading, or if it was the energy from all the crystals in her shop interfering. And if she was a paranormal, did that mean she was an enemy?

She'd studied the shop floor while Morgan had kept the woman talking, to compare the energy trail of Opal to the distinctive energy trail that she'd seen at Amity Jones' house. But, again, her abilities were stunted. Jolene decided to proceed with caution when it came to Opal Mines.

"Dang! We should have asked Opal for a copy of her book," Morgan said after they were settled in the car.

"We could go back and ask, but I'm not really sure we want Opal to know too much about what we're up to. We told her a lot already." Jolene glanced down the street toward Opal's shop. "I don't know if she's friend or foe. Did you get any kind of an intuitive feeling from her?"

Morgan shook her head. "It was hard to get a reading in there. I didn't feel anything except that she might know more than she shared. Maybe all those crystals caused some kind of interference."

"That's what I thought, too," Jolene agreed.

"We could try the library," Fiona suggested. "If you guys think there might be something in the book that could be useful."

"Seems like there should be. Nancy had it in her hand and the killer took it. There must have been a reason for that," Celeste pointed out.

"Good point." Morgan drove the SUV away from the curb. "Where's the library?"

Jolene got out her phone and used voice commands to ask where the library was, then programmed the address into the GPS map system. She directed them three streets over to a tall stone building.

"I'll run in," Fiona said. She hopped out of the car and then leaned back in the window. "I'm starving so let's go for lunch afterwards."

By the time Fiona returned with a shiny new guest library card that the library provided for tourists staying in the area, and the book in her hand, Jolene had found directions to the Rebecca

Nurse house and a cafe on the way to grab some lunch.

Morgan drove to the cafe which was on a street crowded with restaurants. Since it was June and a crystal clear day, most of them had tables set up outside. As they were driving by a Mexican food diner, a familiar dark-haired man caught Jolene's eye.

She whipped around in her seat. "Hey, I think that's Mateo!" She craned her neck to see out the back window of the SUV. They'd driven past, so now all she could see was the back of the man, and the face of his drop-dead gorgeous, long-haired dining companion, the same long hair she'd seen streaming behind the motorcycle. "What would he be doing here?"

Jolene resented the feeling of jealousy that punched at her gut. Mateo had been a mysterious force in her life for several years now. Always coming to her rescue when she needed him most. She'd been attracted to him from the first moment they met, but Jolene wasn't one to go gaga over a man. Even though they weren't dating, she'd always felt there was something special between them so the thought of him eating lunch with a beautiful woman felt like a betrayal.

Morgan angled the rearview mirror to scan the restaurants behind them. "What would be unusual about that? He shows up all the time at strange moments."

"Yeah, but usually he's not having lunch with a beautiful woman." Jolene couldn't keep the emotion out of her voice.

Morgan smirked. "I knew there was something going on with you too. Spill it."

"There's nothing going on. Really. I haven't seen him in months. Not since we got the last relic." Jolene settled back in her seat, her arms crossed. "Honestly, I don't care who he has lunch with."

Jolene was relieved that they were pulling into the cafe parking lot. The moment the car stopped she hopped out, hoping the change of scenery and promise of food would change the topic of conversation.

They sat at a table outdoors under a large umbrella that shaded them from the sun. Jolene tried to relax and enjoy the warm day, delicious smells of their food and the company of her sisters, but her gaze kept stealing out to the street looking for traitorous Mateo.

"So, what's in this book that can help us?" Celeste pushed her salad to the side and flipped the book open on the table. It was a large book, six by nine inches with pages of colored pictures in the middle. She flipped to the pictures, which showed a variety of round crystals.

"Here are some different types of scrying balls." Celeste pointed to one of the pages. "Looks like they come in different sizes but they're all perfectly round."

"So we know we are looking for something round. That ought to narrow it down," Jolene said sarcastically as she crunched on a potato chip.

"And you can see the future in it," Fiona said with a laugh.

Jolene scowled. "You don't really believe that, do you?"

Celeste looked up at her. "It could be true. Look how the stones that Fiona infuses with energy have been able to do magical things."

Jolene chewed another chip. It was true. Fiona had been able to amp up the powers of stones, but those were all stones that had their inherent properties enhanced with energy, like the healing power of carnelian and protective power of obsidian. Seeing the future wasn't an inherent property of any crystal she'd ever heard of.

"It's about as true as witches on broomsticks," Jolene said.

"Maybe the book can tell us more about how to find a real, working scrying ball," Morgan suggested, ignoring Jolene's sour mood.

"Perhaps they emit some special energy or are stored somewhere special or even look special."

Fiona finished her Reuben sandwich, threw her napkin on her plate and reached for the book. "You finish your salad and I'll flip through it."

The girls munched in silence while Fiona thumbed through the book. "This might be something." She read from the book: "Though there's little to differentiate the real scrying ball from ordinary crystal or glass balls, folklore has it that some special scrying balls had a partner—a certain gemstone that would glow with energy indicating the direction of its partner scrying ball."

"The alexandrite gemstone!" Jolene said.

"Yes! It makes perfect sense. The clue we got from Dorian said it would *unlock the path to viewing the future*. I'd wondered what that meant," Morgan said.

Fiona fished the alexandrite gemstone out of her pocket and held it in her palm. It glowed a deep emerald green in the sunlight.

Jolene scrunched up her nose. "It looks like any ordinary alexandrite. I don't see it indicating which path we should take."

Fiona moved her hand around to cover all the directions of a compass. The alexandrite did not change color. "Maybe we have to be closer to the scrying ball?"

"If there even is one," Jolene muttered.

Celeste leveled a look at Jolene. "We know there's something. Some relic we have to find. Probably a scrying ball. Whether it can show the future or not is irrelevant."

"I suppose," Jolene acquiesced. Celeste had a point—their mission was to find the crystal ball. Their employers thought it had some importance that needed to be kept out of the hands of their opponents.

Morgan signaled for the bill. "Possibly, maybe, the alexandrite will give us some kind of indication of what to do when we get to this Rebecca Nurse house."

"We can only hope," Celeste said. "Did you guys remember to order something for Belladonna?"

Jolene grimaced. There would be hell to pay if they didn't come back with a treat for the cat. Belladonna would be mad enough that they'd left her in the hotel room and taken off for the day. If they didn't bring back something delicious, they'd pay with the discovery of hairballs under their pillows or find their favorite sandals clawed to shreds.

"I've got leftover tuna." Morgan indicated for the waiter to get them a takeout box. "I want to get going as soon as possible. Where *are* we going, anyway?"

Jolene checked her phone. "It says the Rebecca Nurse house is in Danvers. Isn't that strange? I thought all the witches were from Salem."

"I think that's just where the trials were," Celeste said. "But if that was her house, then she must not have lived right in Salem."

"I guess you're right." Morgan tapped her finger on the table. Her eyes narrowed and scanned the perimeter, her brows arched in a familiar fashion which usually meant her instincts were on high alert.

"What is it?" Fiona asked.

"I'm not sure, but I feel like someone is watching us."

Jolene sat across from Morgan. She didn't have the intuitive gifts that Morgan did, but sometimes she could pick up intent in people's auras. She turned up her energy awareness to scan the crowd. "I don't see anyone paying attention to us. The energy seems perfectly normal." She twisted in her seat, scanning everything behind her. "Same back here."

"Should we be worried?" Celeste asked.

Morgan relaxed, throwing some bills onto the table and shoving the rest of her tuna sandwich into the Styrofoam container the waiter had dropped off. "No. It was just a passing feeling. It's gone now."

Fiona got up from the table. "It doesn't hurt to be cautious, but we can't go jumping at everything. For all we know, it was just Mateo following us like he usually does."

"Probably. Jolene seems to think she keeps seeing him," Morgan teased.

"You guys are real funny." Jolene wondered if it *was* Mateo following them. She chastised herself for the unwanted hopeful feelings that were bubbling up inside her. Mateo had kissed her several months ago and then he hadn't even bothered to call. He really was the *last* person she wanted to see.

Chapter 9

"I can't believe it's closed!" Celeste stood beside the car, and looked at the red, centuries-old wooden house. Two stories tall, it looked like it had been added to over the years but still kept the basic lines of a colonial house with small windows and a simple design.

"We probably should have checked the hours," Fiona said. "It's closed on Tuesdays."

"That might either be good or bad," Morgan said. "We don't know if we need to look around inside, or if what we seek would be outside."

"And if no one is here to watch us, we can do as we please without making anyone suspicious," Jolene pointed out.

"True," Celeste agreed. "But what if what we need is inside?"

"Well, then that would pose a problem," Jolene admitted. "If the scrying ball is in there, how are we going to get it? It's a museum. We can't just take things from it."

"I doubt it would be inside," Morgan said. "I can't believe this ancient energy-infused relic could be just sitting around in this old witch's house that's now open to the public. After all these years, you would think someone would have taken it."

"Maybe it's protected by a spell," Celeste suggested.

Morgan scoffed. "You don't believe in those, do you?"

Celeste shrugged. "I don't know. I've never known anyone who could cast spells, but you have to admit *our* gifts are a little unusual, so it stands to reason there could be other people with unusual gifts. Like witches who can cast spells."

"If the scrying ball is here, Amity would have found it," Jolene said. "Opal said she made several trips here. Unless it's buried somewhere and she was coming here trying to locate it. Maybe she was digging in different areas for it."

They scanned the ground for signs of recent digging, but there didn't appear to be any.

"I think we might have been led here just to find another clue." Morgan turned to Fiona. "The note said that the keystone would show us the way. Let's dig it out and see what happens."

Fiona took the stone out of her pocket and held it flat in her palm. "It's not doing anything."

"Amity might have gotten the clue. She had the alexandrite stone," Jolene pointed out.

"Maybe, but let's see what we can find out," Morgan said. "We might not be close enough to the clue. We should walk the property. Let's go over to the house."

They walked across the grass toward the house, which was shaded by massive old oak trees on one side. A small garden was next to the house and there was a ridge of pine trees, the edge of a forest, in back.

Jolene rushed ahead, pecking in the windows. "It's really cool in there. Looks just like it did back in the 1600s, I guess."

Fiona followed, pointing the stone at various spots of the house and yard, but none of them made the alexandrite glow any differently. She started around the side of the house.

Celeste saw the stone flash an iridescent pink. "I think you've got something!"

Fiona stopped and moved the stone about, letting it home in on whatever was making it flash. It was a gnarly old tree. Even though it was June and all the trees were lush with new leaves, this tree had none. Its crooked leaf-less limbs jabbed up into the sky ominously.

"It's that tree!" Morgan said excitedly.

"Maybe something's buried beneath it like under the tree behind *Sticks and Stones*." Fiona referred to an old tree behind the shop she shared with Morgan. The shop was an old cottage that had been in their family for centuries. A few years ago, when they first learned about their gifts, they'd followed a similar treasure hunt and one of the clues had been buried beneath the tree.

"That makes sense," Jolene said. "Someone might have used a tree as a place marker."

Jolene, Morgan and Fiona raced toward the tree. They scuffed the dirt around the bottom. Fiona angled the stone toward the thick roots that peeked up from the ground, but the color dimmed instead of deepening.

"It's not working!" Fiona said.

Instead of looking at the base of the tree like her sisters, Celeste was looking at something just beyond the tree—a translucent figure that swirled and shimmered.

A ghost.

"Guys, I don't think it's beneath the tree." Celeste jutted her chin toward the ghost, even though she knew her sisters couldn't see it.

Her sisters were familiar enough with Celeste's gift to know that when they saw her staring into space like that, she was probably looking at a ghost.

"Oh, there's a ghost?" Morgan guessed.

The sisters backed off and let Celeste do her thing. Celeste approached the shimmery figure. It manifested into a more recognizable shape as she got closer. A woman. White bonnet, long skirt with an apron.

"About time you got here," the ghost snapped.

"You've been waiting for us?" Celeste asked.

"You could say that. What took you so long? It seems as if it's been three hundred years."

"Ummm ... We've just now been tasked with finding the scrying ball. Do you know something about it? Who are you?"

"I'm Sarah Easty. I know all about the ball. I was part of the inner circle when the whole thing went down."

"Went down?"

"Yeah, that whole witch hanging thing. What a drag that was. I knew I should've turned that Cotton Mather into a toad when I had the chance."

"You're a witch?" Celeste glanced at Morgan out of the corner of her eye. Maybe Morgan and Jolene would put more stock into spells after this.

"Yes. Well, I *was*. Now I'm just a ghost hanging around waiting for you people to show up and take ownership of the crystal ball."

"That's why we're here. For the crystal ball. Where is it?"

The ghost shimmered, and she appeared to deflate before Celeste's eyes, her image becoming more translucent. "Well, see, that's the problem. I don't know where it is. I was hanged before I could find out where Sam put it."

"Sam?"

"Sam Gooding. He was one of us. He was one of the few not accused of being a witch, so it was up to him to protect the scrying ball. It's special, you know. Infused with energy from the ancients. And if it falls into the wrong hands ... well ..." she waved her ghostly hands in the air frantically. "I don't need to tell you what will happen then."

"No, we're well aware of what will happen. So, how can we find it?" The keystone had led them to the ghost, so Celeste knew that she would provide them with a vital clue whether she knew it or not. Since Celeste was the only one who could talk to the ghost, it fell on her try to figure out what exactly that clue was. She was glad she was getting a chance to use her unique gift to help find the relic. She just hoped she was asking the right questions.

"The plan was for Sam to hide it and leave a clue to its whereabouts."

"Okay. Do you know where this clue is?"

Sarah winced. "No."

This wasn't getting them anywhere. Celeste realized she'd have to take another tack. "Just what does this scrying ball look like?"

"Oh, it's about this big around and it's clear." Sarah moved her hands to mimic the size of a small honeydew melon.

"And where do you think Sam would hide it? In his house? Or somewhere else?"

"Well, there weren't many places to hide things here in 1692. And none of us knew if we were going to make it out alive. You see, a lot of people were being accused of witchcraft and not all of them were witches, either. But I do recall him saying that he would sketch out a clue for future generations."

"Sketch? Like in a painting or drawing?"

Sarah started to become agitated. "That, I'm not sure about. They came for me before we could exchange the information." Sarah swirled and dipped, mist dripped off her onto the ground as she darted looks out onto the street. "Oh, no. They're coming for me again!"

"What? No. We don't hang people for witchcraft anymore."

But Sarah wasn't paying attention to Celeste. Her eyes widened and she pointed to something behind Celeste's shoulder. "There they are!"

Celeste whirled around and saw a police car stopping before the house. When she turned back, Sarah's ghost was gone.

Detective Peterson didn't seem the least bit happy to see them. He scowled, his eyes drifting from one sister to the next, then over to the house as if looking to see if they'd done any damage. "What are you ladies doing here?"

"Oh, you know. Tourist stuff." Morgan gestured to indicate the house and yard.

Peterson cocked his head to one side. "The museum is closed."

"Yes, we saw the sign," Jolene said. "Who would think it would be closed on a Tuesday?"

"We'd come all the way here so we thought we'd just look around," Fiona added.

Peterson looked up at the dead tree they were standing under. "Uh-huh."

"Have you arrested anyone for Nancy Baumann's murder?" Celeste asked. "I hate to think of a killer running around loose."

"No. In fact, you ladies are my prime suspects."

"What?"

Peterson shrugged. "Look at things from my perspective. It's mighty strange that you four suddenly appear in town, find a dead body and are now discovered trespassing at the museum here after hours."

"Surely you don't think we had anything to do with her death?"

Peterson cracked a smile. "No, probably not. I don't see as you ladies have a motive. Plus, I do have to admit there have been some strange goings-on lately, before you arrived in town."

"Strange goings-on? With Nancy?" Morgan asked.

"No, with Amity Jones."

"You mean she died of suspicious causes?"

Peterson's eyes narrowed. "What makes you say that?"

"Oh, nothing. It's just that *you* said something was suspicious," Morgan pointed out.

He brushed his hands through his buzz cut. "Oh, right. Yep, she was an odd one. Just what was your business with her, anyway?"

"We told you," Fiona said. "We bought some crystals and wanted to follow up on them."

"Oh, right. And why are you still hanging around town?"

"Tourist stuff, like we said. We know about the Salem witch trials and always wanted to tour some of the museums and houses. That's why we're here. We didn't know this was closed today."

"Sure looks like you were making yourselves at home." Peterson nodded toward Celeste who stood on the opposite side of the tree. "And what's she doing way over there? Looks kind of strange. Like you're up to something."

"Oh, I'm an amateur arborist. I love trees and these are some real old ones." Celeste touched the old, gnarled tree with her hand. "And this one here is just so interesting. I just wanted to get a closer look. But now that I've done that we can go."

"That's a smart idea. Don't want to see you getting into any trouble around here. You know, they say there are witches and ghosts everywhere." Peterson winked at the girls as he turned back toward his car.

Celeste laughed. "Oh, we don't believe in witches and ghosts."

"Just as well. Then you ladies better move along. Just so you know, it can be dangerous out here at night." He indicated the nearby woods. "I wouldn't want to have to answer a call about you being in trouble."

"Thanks, that's good advice!" The girls waved as they got into the SUV and Morgan drove out onto the road. Celeste glanced into the side view mirror as they drove away. She saw Peterson leaning against the front of his car, his arms folded across his chest, watching them go.

"Well, that explains that," Morgan said.

"What?" Celeste asked.

"The feeling I had that someone was following us. I guess it must've been Peterson."

"You think? But why? He can't seriously suspect we killed Nancy. He was probably just doing his rounds and saw us here," Fiona said. "It *is* closed so I guess we were technically trespassing"

"I don't think he was doing rounds. He's a detective who responded to our call when we found Nancy in Salem." Jolene pointed to the 'Entering Salem' sign they were just passing. "And the Rebecca Nurse house is in Danvers, which is out of his jurisdiction. Right?"

Chapter 10

Belladonna greeted them at their hotel room door with a smug look on her face that made Jolene worry about what the cat had been up to while they were gone.

"We brought you back a treat." Morgan held up the white Styrofoam box.

Belladonna circled her, looking up with innocent, ice blue eyes. "*Meow.*" She let out her softest cry.

Now Jolene was sure the cat was up to something.

Morgan picked the flakes of tuna fish out of her sandwich and put them in the cat's feed bowl while Belladonna watched patiently, her whiskers twitching as the salty smell of the fish wafted into the room.

"What do you think she did while we were gone?" Fiona asked as she peered into the adjoining rooms to assess the damage.

"Who knows? She usually doesn't stay put. I'm surprised we didn't find her out at the Rebecca Nurse house," Celeste joked.

"Speaking of which, we need to figure out what we should do next," Fiona said.

Celeste had told them about her conversation with Sarah Easty's ghost while they were in the car on the way home. They agreed that finding out as much as they could about Sam Gooding was a good plan.

Jolene flipped her laptop open. "I'll do some research online. Maybe I can find out more about this Sam Gooding guy."

While Jolene tapped on the keyboard, Belladonna circled the bowl that Morgan had put on the floor. The cat sniffed it from all angles and looked at the girls suspiciously as if she suspected they might put something less than healthy in her bowl. Finally, she settled onto her haunches and started daintily licking the fish.

"I can't really find much. I can see his name in old town records, but nothing associated with the witch trials. No newspaper articles." Jolene looked up from the computer and held her hands up in surrender. "There's really not much on him."

"There has to be something useful," Celeste said. "That was the only lead I got from the ghost."

"We have to act. We know there are others looking for this scrying ball and at least one person's been killed over it," Fiona added.

"Maybe two, if Amity's death wasn't as natural as it appeared," Jolene said.

"That's true. It could've been by paranormal means because those can look like heart attacks." Fiona pointed at the book on crystals. "The killer took this book from Nancy, so now he knows what we do, that we're looking for a scrying ball *and* that the alexandrite gemstone will show us the way."

"And if he knows we have the keystone, we could be next on his list," Celeste said.

Morgan shifted restlessly in her chair. "Yes, of course we could be in danger. That's nothing new, but I felt like we were followed and, in fact, that feeling, and one of being watched ... it's getting closer."

"*Meow*!" Belladonna jerked her head up from the bowl and trotted over to the door. Four pairs of eyes followed her and watched as she sniffed the crack at the bottom of the door.

"Do you think someone could be out there?" Jolene whispered as she slowly got up and crept to the door.

"Maybe, but who?" Morgan whispered back as she, Fiona and Celeste readied themselves for a fight.

"Could be anyone. The cop. The person who killed Nancy. Opal Mines or whatever paranormal Dr. Bly has sent." Jolene reached for the doorknob.

Belladonna's meowing got louder.

Jolene whipped the door open.

Standing in hall, his fist raised to knock on their door was a handsome, dark-haired man with velvety brown eyes. Mateo.

Jolene's heart melted at the sight of him. Then her eyes narrowed and her heart hardened when she remembered seeing him with the long-haired beauty. "What are you doing here?"

The smile that broke down her heart's defenses bloomed across his face. *Used* to break down her defenses, she reminded her heart. Jolene indicated for him to enter.

"I heard you guys were in town so I decided to come visit you." Mateo took a seat on the couch, his long legs stretched out in front of him. He winked at Jolene, who crossed her arms and went to the opposite side of the room.

"What are you doing in town?" Fiona asked.

Mateo shrugged. "I spend a lot of time here. This is a great town. And, of course, I heard about the note you got from Dorian so I wanted to come by and see if I could help. Why don't you bring me up to speed?"

Morgan, Fiona and Celeste took turns filling him in while Jolene brooded silently on the other side of the room.

"Sounds like you need to find out more about this Sam guy." Mateo turned to Jolene. "Were you able to dig anything up on the Internet?"

89

"No. I think any records of him are too old to have made their way online."

Mateo nodded thoughtfully. "I might know of a place where you can find out more. If he was involved, even remotely, with the witch trials, they may have information about him at the Salem Ephemera Museum."

"What is that?" Fiona asked.

"It's a museum here in town. It's actually just a few streets over from this hotel. Hardly anyone goes there because ... well, it's not exactly that exciting. There aren't any wax figure displays or antiques. It's all paper. All kinds of documents from the 1600s onward. Anything to do with the Salem witch trials is in there."

"Sounds like it's worth a shot." Fiona looked at her sisters, all of whom nodded.

"How do you know so much about this area anyway?" Morgan asked.

Mateo smiled as he got up from the couch. "Let's just say I have an 'in'. Speaking of which, I know an awesome place to go for dinner. He turned to Jolene. "Would you join me?"

Panic welled up inside her. Jolene's eyes flicked from Morgan to Celeste to Fiona and back to Mateo. "We haven't discussed our dinner plans."

Mateo's left brow rose and he looked at the other girls, who all had smirks on their faces.

"I'm skipping supper. I ate too much ice cream the other day and I need to cut back." Fiona's eyes sparkled with mischief.

"I'm relaxing in the tub, gonna eat take-out and call Luke." Morgan's wore a smug smile that made Jolene want to punch her.

"I'm not eating either." Celeste started toward her room. "I need to go for a jog."

"Looks like you're in need of some company for supper." Mateo took Jolene's hand and pulled her gently toward the door before she could protest. She left with Mateo, looking back just in time to see her sisters' knowing smirks.

As Mateo led her down the hall, Jolene's heart couldn't decide whether to sink in despair or rise in hope.

***

Mateo did, indeed, know a nice little restaurant. They sat outdoors because he knew Jolene loved dining outside. It was dusk, the low light casting pleasant shadows on the ground and accentuating the angular lines of Mateo's handsome face. They ate companionably, sticking to hushed talk of paranormal skills and filling each other in on what had passed since they'd last seen each other.

Jolene fought off the feeling of closeness she usually felt when she was with him. She wasn't sure she wanted to feel that way.

She noticed him studying her as if he sensed something was off. It made her nervous. Too nervous to enjoy her meal of baked haddock and mashed potatoes. She pushed the food from one side of her gold-rimmed china plate to the other, which was unusual. Usually, she ate like a horse.

Jolene realized she was being immature to feel so insecure and standoffish because of the other woman. Mateo had never made any promises to her. Heck, they weren't even dating. But she still had no desire to share him with anyone. She was a one-man kind of gal.

When they finished eating, Mateo paid the bill and took hold of her hand. They walked slowly back to the hotel hand in hand. The night was warm, the air perfumed with honeysuckle. A slight breeze kicked up from the ocean four streets over and ruffled her hair. Mateo's hand was comforting and Jolene's heart leapt when he interlaced his fingers with hers.

"I just want to make sure that you girls realize that whoever else is looking for this relic could be very powerful." Mateo studied her with concerned eyes.

"I think we know what we're doing by now," she said.

"I know you do. But I might not always be there to protect you."

Jolene snorted. "Why? Do you have someone else to protect now?" She hated the catty way that sounded but once it was out it was too late to take it back.

Mateo's brow furrowed. "What are you talking about?"

"Nothing. Never mind."

Mateo stopped and turned to face her. "I have a lot of missions that I do for the paranormal society, but none is closer to my heart than protecting you and your sisters. Especially you. But you've proven that you can take care of yourselves, so now I have to go on other missions and can't be around as much."

"Right. Of course. I don't expect you to be around all the time." Her heart stuttered as his hands made their way from her shoulders down her arms. Was he getting closer? Her breath caught as his head dipped toward hers.

"Ahahaha!"

"*Hiss.*"

Jolene jerked her attention from Mateo's lips to see what looked like the edge of a black cape and the tip of a broom disappearing around the corner. The fluffy black cat with the golden eyes sat in the street, hissing in the direction of the cape. "Did you see that?"

Mateo looked over his shoulder. "What?"

"I thought I saw a black dress or a cape and a ..." Jolene realized how stupid it sounded but she said it anyway, "broomstick."

"Someone sweeping?"

"Umm, not exactly." The broomstick was flying.

The black cat came to them and rubbed up against Mateo's leg. Mateo bent down and scratched the cat's ear then went to look down the alley. "Kitty, do you see someone over there?"

Jolene followed him, peering around the corner to see ... nothing. "There's no one. I must have imagined it."

"No broomstick or black capes. I know this is Salem, but I don't think there are any witches flying around on broomsticks tonight," Mateo teased.

"Of course not." Jolene shrugged. "I don't believe in witches, anyway."

Mateo turned serious. "Don't worry, you will."

Chapter 11

The next day, the sisters drove to the Salem Ephemera Museum, even though it was so close that they could have easily walked. They had high hopes they might get a hot lead and would need the SUV to check it out.

Jolene was unusually quiet on the ride over. She was tired, having spent most of the night alternating between mooning over the interrupted kiss and chastising herself for wanting to be kissed in the first place.

In a way, she was glad the kiss had been interrupted. Even though she'd desperately wanted to kiss Mateo at the time, now, in the light of day, she realized she'd be better off if she didn't get involved, despite the magnetic pull she felt whenever she was in his orbit.

Besides, she had an important job to do that would require all of her attention. She pushed the annoying thoughts of Mateo and his kiss out of her head as Morgan parked their SUV in front of the museum.

The building was a boxy rectangle of gray cement, nothing fancy or flashy. Located on a side street, it was not near any of the other tourist attractions. Its plain, small sign hung over the door.

Inside, Jolene smelled the musty aroma of centuries-old paper. Antique oak display cases ringed the perimeter of the small front room. Protected behind the beveled glass of the cases sat old crumbling diaries, yellowed newspapers with flaking edges and tattered letters, the ink barely visible.

The shuffle of footsteps sounded from the back and Jolene looked up to see an elderly man come around the corner, his eyes widening as he noticed them.

"Welcome! Welcome! I'm Henry Oaks, museum curator. I have to say, I don't get many visitors. In fact, you're lucky you caught me in. I just got back from my walk. Well, really it's more of a shuffle. I like to do a few blocks twice a day. Try to keep myself fit." He threw his bony shoulders back and rubbed his sunken chest as if to emphasize how fit he was. "It's a pleasure to see someone enjoying the displays."

"Thanks. We love learning about history." Morgan pointed to one of the taller display cases that housed diaries propped up on stands, their fragile pages open to the middle. "We're particularly interested in old diaries."

"Oh, yes." Henry waved his hand toward another case. We have plenty of those. And some in the back still to be catalogued. Though mostly the back is filled with old newspapers."

Fiona glanced toward the doorway to the back. "Oh, there's more?"

"Not for public display. There's a lot of cataloging left to be done. People are always dropping off stuff they find in their attics and it's up to me to make sure they get recorded properly." Henry straightened, his chest puffing out proudly. "You know, we have the largest collection of Salem witch ephemera in the country."

"We heard," Celeste said. "That's why we came."

"Yes. We heard you were something of an expert who would be able to tell us all about the various people involved with the Salem witch trials." Jolene knew her sisters were trying to act nonchalant, but sometimes she just wished they would cut to the chase.

He regarded her with narrowed eyes. "Well, I know more than most, I suppose. Who did you want to know about in particular?"

"Sam Gooding."

Henry pursed his lips together and looked up at the ceiling. "Sam Gooding. Can't say as I recall that name." He shuffled over to a large

98

mahogany desk where an ancient computer with a monitor as big as a Volkswagen Beetle sat. He tapped on the keys with thick fingers. "Let's see if I've catalogued anything from this Gooding person."

The sisters drifted over to stand behind him, Jolene looking over his shoulder, memorizing everything she saw on the screen. She had a photographic memory and you never knew when information might come in handy.

"Oh, yes." He straightened with a crack of his spine. "There is something in back. It was catalogued last summer. I'll be right back."

Henry shuffled off and the sisters busied themselves by looking at the displays. Though most of the paper was yellowed and flaky, Jolene was amazed that any three hundred-year-old paper still existed.

She was busy reading a diary of one of the young girls who accused a witch of causing her seizures when Henry returned with an armful of rolled up papers, a long cylinder and a thick, three-ring binder.

He put the papers on top of the glass display case. "Why are you girls so interested in this person?"

"Term paper," Jolene lied.

"Oh, you girls are students?" He eyed them suspiciously. Jolene was young enough to be a student, but Morgan and Fiona were past thirty. Henry must have realized they were a little too old. "College?"

"Just me." Jolene waved at the others. "These are my sisters. They just came along for the ride."

"Okay. Well, this here was brought in by someone who found it in an old trunk at an auction. These are photocopies, of course. It's some clothing and a diary. In here," he tapped the binder, "is the information on Sam that was dug up by the intern earlier this year. Turns out *I* didn't log this in. I was on vacation. That's why I didn't remember him."

Jolene bent over to study the documents. Pictures of a rotted vest, pants and shirt. There was also a picture of a leather book, presumably the diary. The binder contained information about the birth certificate, death certificate, and newspaper clippings.

"We were looking for some paintings or drawings that he did," Jolene said.

Henry flipped through the binder. "I don't see anything about that. Was he an artist?"

"We're not sure. Are you sure there's nothing in there? Maybe in his diary?"

"These are photocopies of everything we got. Some of the diary pages are here." Henry leafed to the back of the binder.

Jolene felt disappointed. Nothing stuck out from what she'd seen. Maybe more would be revealed upon further study. "Can I check this information out and take it home?"

Henry's brow creased. "Check it out? No, we don't allow that."

"Can we make photocopies?" Morgan asked.

"Nope, sorry. Don't allow that, either. Museum policy. If we let people do that, we'd have to buy a new machine every month. I'm afraid you'll have to stay here and read it all. You can take notes."

Henry grabbed a feather duster and started running it over the display cases while the sisters huddled over the papers.

"I didn't bring anything to take notes, but we can take pictures with our phones," Celeste suggested.

"Yeah, but not all of it. Let's pick out the important stuff," Morgan said.

Jolene's chest tightened in frustration. "I think this is a wild goose chase. Are you sure you got the right information?" she asked Celeste.

"Yes. Maybe it's buried in here and we need to look through it more thoroughly."

Jolene glanced over at Henry, who turned quickly back to his task. She lowered her voice. "If he wasn't a known artist, then I think the diary is probably our best bet." Jolene flipped through the photocopied pages. She didn't need to take a picture. She knew from past experience she would remember exactly what was on each page.

Morgan got busy taking pictures of the newspaper articles. Fiona started on the pile of photocopies.

Jolene felt her energy spike as she flipped the pages. The diary copies had an energy stamp, dark energy, which was strange, because these were just photocopies. It must be pretty strong if it could imprint onto a copy of the original.

Sam must have been an incredibly powerful paranormal, which made sense because he was tasked with caring for the scrying ball ... but why would his energy be dark? Maybe an imprint on a photocopy reversed the energy, kind of like how a negative of a picture was reversed.

Jolene was just about to mention this to her sisters when she turned the page to reveal a feathery sketch. It looked like a living room with a fireplace on one side and a wide stairway next to it. Sam's house? And what better place to hide a crystal ball than in your own home.

"Look," she whispered, pointing to the page.

"A sketch," Celeste whispered. "Sarah said he would sketch out a clue."

Morgan snapped a shot even though Jolene already had the sketch committed to memory. She glanced back to make sure Henry was still busy dusting. He was clear on the other side of the room so she leaned forward and said in a low whisper, "This could be the very place where he hid the crystal ball."

Morgan nodded, checking her phone to be sure she'd captured the image. "Now all we have to do is figure out exactly where *this* is."

Chapter 12

"Do you think Amity knew about the sketch?" Morgan held up her phone with the picture of the sketch to show her sisters. They were all seated in their parked SUV before the Museum.

"I don't think so. At least not from the Ephemera Museum because Henry didn't know about Sam. He'd never shown this to anyone," Fiona said.

"He didn't even know it had been logged in, though. Maybe whoever logged it in showed her," Celeste suggested.

"Whether she knew about it or not doesn't really help us." Jolene turned to Celeste. "Are you sure Sarah Easty's ghost didn't give you any idea of where Sam might have hidden it?"

"The ghost didn't, but Opal said Amity kept talking about that Rebecca Nurse house. Maybe it's in there?"

Jolene pressed her lips together. "We've already been there. That's where we got the clue about Sam, from Sarah's ghost. It doesn't seem like there could be *another* clue there, does it?"

"Maybe not outside, but we haven't been inside," Morgan said. "We've got nothing to lose checking it out."

"Good point." Fiona reached into her pocket and pulled out the alexandrite gemstone. She held it flat in her palm as she waved her hand slowly in different directions. The stone just sat there glowing a dull green.

"Well that thing is no help," Celeste said

"Maybe, I need to point it in the direction of the clue for it to take effect," Fiona said. "Which direction is the Rebecca Nurse house?"

Jolene checked her navigational app then pointed behind them. "That way."

Fiona moved her hand in that direction and the stone gave a little flash of yellow then back to dull green. "That wasn't much of a sign, but I guess it won't hurt to head back out there."

Morgan put the car in gear and they drove the ten minutes to Danvers. The grounds looked much different than they had the day before. Today, the museum was open and there were cars parked in the lot and people milling about.

Jolene noticed, with amusement, that many of the museum employees were dressed in colonial garb. She amped up her gifts as the sisters walked toward the house, hoping she would notice a shift in energy. If the crystal ball was inside, maybe it would be emitting some sort of telltale energy vibe.

Jolene had already peeked in the window when they were there the previous day, so the utilitarian furnishings and colonial ambience were no surprise. The house was decorated with plain furniture, unadorned walls and wide pine floors. It smelled of old wood and wood oil and long ago fires. A large brick fireplace, similar to the one in the sketch caught her eye. It was a giant hearth complete with large cooking pots hanging on a metal bar, but it wasn't exactly the same. For one thing, the fireplace in Sam Gooding's sketch had stairs near it. This one didn't.

Morgan had her phone out and was doing a similar comparison. "I don't think this matches."

"No, it doesn't. Are you getting any kind of vibe?" Jolene asked.

Morgan shook her head. "You?"

"Nope."

The girls made a quick tour of the rest of the house, including watching a woman sew a quilt while another put the finishing touches on an apple pie. The smell of sugar, cinnamon and apples made Jolene's stomach rumble.

"I guess apple pie smelled just as good back in the 1600s as it does today," Celeste commented as they made their way out the front door.

"Which reminds me, I'm hungry," Jolene said.

"Me, too," Fiona and Morgan said at the same time, then laughed and tapped knuckles. "Jinx."

"I vote we go find some place to have lunch and decide what to do next," Celeste suggested.

"Just a minute." Fiona pulled the alexandrite stone out of her pocket and aimed it back toward the Rebecca Nurse house. It didn't light up. The girls looked at each other in disappointment.

"I guess this was a false lead," Morgan said. "Maybe the sketch isn't even what Sarah's ghost was talking about, Celeste."

Celeste glanced over to the tree where she'd talked to the ghost the previous afternoon. "I don't know. I wish she'd come and tell us, but I don't see anything. Probably she wouldn't manifest with all these people around. Maybe we should come back after it closes."

"And risk the ire of Detective Unfriendly?" Fiona joked.

Morgan laughed. "Hopefully he's not following us twenty-four seven ... though I do have to admit, I keep getting a sneaking suspicion we're being watched." Her eyes drifted over to a wooded area.

Jolene looked in that direction. Something caught her eye. "It looks like there's an old family cemetery back there. Maybe your ghost is hanging out there, Celeste?"

A family with two small children was just coming back from the graveyard. No one else was there, which afforded them a perfect opportunity to go talk to a ghost.

"Can't hurt to try." Celeste headed in that direction, followed by her sisters.

The small graveyard was in a grove of pine trees, which were home to several twittering birds and a chipmunk that rustled through the leaves and pine needles, stuffing his cheeks with pine nuts.

The perimeter of the cemetery was marked by tall granite posts. A monument to Rebecca Nurse sat smack dab in the middle. Everyone looked at Celeste, who shook her head. No ghost was present.

Fiona took the alexandrite keystone out and aimed it around the graveyard. When she hit the southeasterly quadrant, it blinked orange and yellow. "Something is over there."

She held it out in her palm like a compass and they walked in that direction, stopping over an old slate gravestone. The stone was engraved with a weeping willow and an epitaph in script that was impossible to read due to the abundance of moss and lichen on the face of the heavily worn stone.

But one thing was easy to read—the name: Dorcas Gooding.

"Gooding! A relative of Sam's?" Celeste asked.

Fiona aimed the alexandrite at the gravestone and the gemstone glowed hot orange. When she aimed it in a different direction, the glow dimmed. "I bet she is."

"And I bet this is a clue," Jolene added.

"Why would she be buried in the Nurse family graveyard?" Morgan took out her phone and started scrolling through the pictures of the material from the museum. She stopped at one and used her pinched fingers to make the screen bigger. "They were related. Dorcas Gooding was married to a relative of Rebecca Nurse."

"That's it! That's the clue," Celeste said.

"It's good to know the alexandrite works at ferreting out the clues," Fiona added.

"Just like the note said, it will *show us the path.*" Morgan's voice was soft.

Jolene looked from the text on Morgan's screen to the glowing gemstone. "That's great, but it still doesn't tell us where Sam hid the crystal ball. If the clue was the epitaph, it's unreadable now."

Chapter 13

After lunch, they drove back to the hotel, passing the restaurant Jolene had eaten at with Mateo the previous night. As Jolene's gaze lingered on the table where they'd sat, she felt hollow, empty. After the kiss had been interrupted, Jolene had made the excuse that she needed to get to bed early. Mateo had delivered her safely to the hotel then gone away.

Where was he now? She hadn't heard from him. Was she expecting to? What *was* she expecting?

As they turned onto the street of their hotel, she noticed the same fluffy black cat that had been present the night before hanging around the corner of the building. Could it be the same cat from Amity Jones' house?

"I hope Belladonna doesn't see that cat hanging around outside the hotel. She'll be jealous," Fiona said.

"Or make friends with it," Morgan joked.

"Let's hope we don't have to bring it home with us." Celeste narrowed her eyes at it as they got out of the car. "Is that the same cat we saw in the woods next to Amity's house?"

Jolene looked back at the cat. The one in the woods had glowing, golden eyes. She couldn't see the eyes on this cat. It had turned its back on them and was trotting away down the alley.

Fiona said, "That's funny. Come to think of it, there was one in the mystical shop, *The Eye of Newt*, where we bought the alexandrite stone."

"Pfft." Morgan waved her hand in the air. "There are plenty of black cats around. It's not like they're rare."

"Speaking of cats, we forgot to get something for Belladonna from the restaurant." Jolene grimaced.

"Shoot. She'll just have to eat her cat food," Celeste said.

"Oh, boy. She's not gonna like that. She'll have it in for us," Fiona laughed.

Morgan opened the door to their suite to find Belladonna sitting on the windowsill, her gaze fixed on something below.

"What's out there?" Morgan picked up Belladonna and cuddled her while looking out the window. The black cat was below looking up. "You see the other kitty. No, you can't go out and play with the kitty."

"*Merow*!" Belladonna wiggled out of Morgan's arms, twisted in the air and made a perfect landing on all four legs, then she swished her tail and padded over to the kitchenette.

"I guess she told you," Fiona said.

"I told you she'd be mad that we didn't bring her a treat." Jolene fished in the cabinet for one of the cans of cat food they'd brought with them. She picked out turkey and gravy—Belladonna's favorite.

"So, what do we do now?" Celeste asked as Jolene dumped the smelly food into Belladonna's dish.

"I guess more research needs to be done," Morgan said. "I'll call Luke and see if he's heard anything new."

"Good idea." Celeste grabbed her purse from the couch and rummaged inside it. "I'll call Cal. Maybe I can have him do some research on Gooding. He might know something about the Salem witch trials or the people involved."

Cal Reid had been a close family friend for many years and more recently he'd become Celeste's boyfriend. He ran an antique and pawnshop in Maine and was an expert in antiquities. The sisters often called upon his expertise to help in their adventures.

"That's a good idea. I'll call Jake and make sure he's not missing your assistance." Fiona winked at Jolene.

Fiona's boyfriend, Jake Cooper, a former Noquitt cop, had recently opened his own private detective agency. Jolene worked with him using her computer skills to help on their cases, but with Jolene in Salem Jake was having to fend for himself.

Jolene secretly hoped that he *did* miss her assistance, thus proving how invaluable she was to the business. She'd had to fight to move up from 'assistant' status to field work. She wanted Jake to realize she was good enough to be a full P.I. partner.

Jolene did a mental eye roll while her sisters got on their phones, their eyes bright and sparkly as they whispered to their boyfriends. She pulled out the closest thing she had to a boyfriend—her computer—and pushed away annoying thoughts of Mateo.

"You guys carry on with your conversations, don't mind me. I'll just research this Sam guy a little bit more." As Jolene tapped away on the keys, she reviewed the museum papers in her mind. Looking for ideas or some kind of clue as to where Sam Gooding might have hidden the crystal ball.

Belladonna finished her meal and hopped up onto the desk, skidding on the papers that had accumulated there.

"Did you like your supper?" Jolene scratched her behind the ears.

"*Merow.*" Belladonna batted at the pile and a few pieces of paper fell on the floor.

"Hey, now. I know we made a mess but that's no reason to throw things around." Jolene bent down and picked up the papers then piled them on top of the desk, straightening the piles into neat stacks.

"*Merowww*!!" Belladonna batted more papers off.

"Maybe that means she didn't like her supper," Fiona, who had just ended her call, suggested. "Jake says he has a new job for you when we get back."

"He can't run the place without me, can he?" Jolene teased.

Fiona laughed. "Well, he didn't say as much but we can always read between the lines."

"*Meowww.*" Belladonna slid around the desk, pushing off some of the smaller papers then sat smack dab in the middle of the 1692 reproduction map of Salem Village.

"Yep, she's mad," Morgan said.

"Did Luke have any new news?" Jolene asked.

"He verified what Mateo said about Bly having someone with paranormal gifts looking for the relic, which is the crystal ball." Morgan shrugged. "But that's not anything we didn't expect. He didn't have any new information, so it looks like we have to work with what we've got.

Celeste came in from her room, clicking her phone shut. "Cal said the witch thing wasn't his expertise and he doesn't know anyone. So he wasn't much help, either."

"*Mew.*"

"Looks like Belladonna agrees." Jolene gently pushed the cat off the desk.

"*Meroooow*!" Belladonna jumped back up.

Jolene rolled her eyes and craned her neck to look around Belladonna at Morgan, Fiona and Celeste. "So, all we know is Sarah Easty's ghost said that Sam Gooding had the crystal ball in 1692 and he was supposed to hide it. I actually think Sam might have been a paranormal because I got a strange vibe when we were looking through the papers at the Ephemera Museum."

Morgan said, "Amity Jones must've been onto something because she was asking about crystals and she was at the Rebecca Nurse house."

"That's according to Opal, but we don't know if she's friend or foe at this point. She could have been just telling us that about Amity to throw us off track," Fiona suggested.

"*Mew*." Belladonna flopped down on the map and rolled over on her back.

Celeste scratched Belladonna's belly. "We also know that Sam was related to Rebecca Nurse through marriage."

Fiona took out the alexandrite gemstone. "We also have this that will somehow show us the next clue, except we need to get close enough to that clue so the keystone can pick up its energy and point it out to us."

"I'm pretty sure the scrying ball is not at the Rebecca Nurse house," Morgan said. "Even though we have found a few clues there so far, my intuition tells me that is not where it is."

"*Merup*!" Belladonna leapt up from the table, pushing all the papers off including the map which floated down to the floor.

Jolene bent down to pick it up and then it hit her. "Wait a minute. It makes sense that Sam didn't hide the scrying ball at the Rebecca Nurse house because they were already accusing witches when they realized the ball needed to be protected. Rebecca was already accused, but Sam wasn't accused of being a warlock."

"That's right. I didn't think of that," Morgan said. "They wouldn't want the crystal ball at the house of someone being accused of witchcraft."

Jolene put the map back on the desk. "So, if he didn't hide it at her house, he might have hidden it at *his*." She tapped her index finger on the map. "And now, all we have to do is figure out exactly *where* his house was."

Chapter 14

The next morning, Jolene awoke early, made some coffee and double-checked all their information. They'd worked well into the night, amidst much meowing and paper-throwing by Belladonna, going through all the pictures they'd taken of the museum's paperwork.

They finally got a lead on Sam Gooding's address and discovered it was only a few blocks from the hotel, very near to the Ephemera Museum, at Number Two West Great River Road. Jolene had tried to double check the address by hacking into the town's database and accessing the town records, but they didn't go back that far.

"*Meow*." Belladonna paced by the door expectantly.

"No, you can't go."

The cat slitted her eyes, slicing an angry glare in Jolene's direction.

"It's for your own good."

"*Merow*!" Belladonna spun around, presented her backside to Jolene, flicked her tail and stalked off.

"What was that all about?" Fiona emerged from her room, looking refreshed in a gray t-shirt and cropped leg jeans, her long hair tied back in a ponytail.

"She wanted to come with us."

Morgan appeared at her door similarly dressed, but with a black t-shirt. "It's bad enough we let her roam free when we aren't here. The hotel manager is going to catch on. I've already noticed him giving us the hairy eyeball."

Jolene stretched in her chair. "Hopefully, we won't be here much longer. We don't have much for breakfast."

"I have my stuff. I'm starving." Celeste appeared in the doorway, stifling a yawn. She helped herself to her health food, leaving the coffee for her sisters.

Fiona said, "We can get some breakfast when we're out. She winked at Jolene. "If you're lucky, I'll even buy you that ice cream I owe you for dessert."

Celeste glanced out the window while eating her cottage cheese. "It's a beautiful day today. We should walk. We've been eating out a lot we need to walk off the calories."

Jolene added hopefully, "Especially if ice cream is in our future."

"*Mew*." Belladonna trotted over to the door.

"Not you, Belladonna." Morgan's words received an angry slit-eyed glare from the cat.

Soon after Fiona asked, "Are you all ready?" She walked over to the door and grabbed the knob. Belladonna pushed in between her legs so she could run out. "Oh, no, not you. We'll bring you back an ice cream."

"She's not going to let us leave." Celeste pulled a bag of cat treats from the kitchen drawer and crinkled it noisily. "We can distract her with these."

Belladonna's attention flicked between the door and the treats.

Celeste took three treats out while Fiona, Jolene and Morgan lined up by the door at the ready.

"Ready?" Celeste held the treats up and looked to Fiona.

Fiona nodded.

Celeste threw the treats toward the window.

Belladonna whipped her head around, taking off after the treats at high speed, a flash of white across the floor, then she leapt up and caught one treat in mid-air.

At the same time, Fiona ripped the door open and the girls bolted out of the room.

Belladonna jerked her attention over to the door just as Celeste, who was last in line, slipped out. The cat spun on a dime and ran for the door, but she wasn't fast enough. Celeste pulled the door shut just as Belladonna leaped for it.

Jolene grimaced as she heard the frustrated yowling behind the door. "We better bring her back something extra special for that."

"You can say that again," Morgan said as Belladonna's muffled cries of anger followed them down the hallway.

Jolene was glad they had decided to walk because it was a perfect June day. The temperature was already in the mid-seventies, cool enough for walking but pleasant enough not to need a jacket. Dots of sun beamed through the thick leaves of the trees overhead and danced on the sidewalk. Seagulls cried in the distance.

"So what's going on with you and Mateo, anyway? Morgan asked.

The question was out of the blue, but Jolene wasn't surprised. She'd been expecting a barrage of questions from her sisters after she'd gone to dinner with him the other night.

"Nothing, really." It was pretty much the truth.

"What do you mean nothing?" Fiona asked. "It doesn't seem like nothing to me."

Jolene shrugged. "I don't really know what's going on. Honestly, I haven't thought about it much. I've been focused on finding the crystal ball.

You know, saving the world from evil and all. I think that's a little bit more important than thinking about my non-relationship with the mysterious Mateo."

"Well, you can still—"

"*Meow!*"

They all stopped short and spun around, expecting to find Belladonna behind them. But it wasn't Belladonna. It was the black fluffy cat.

"There are a lot of black cats around here," Celeste said.

"Well, it *is* Salem," Fiona replied.

"Hey, this is the street." Jolene pointed up at the street sign for West Great River Road. She turned the corner and her heart sank.

"There are no homes here," said Celeste, the master of stating the obvious.

"No. Number two is a pharmacy." Morgan stopped on the sidewalk in front of the pharmacy.

Jolene double-checked her notes, and then the GPS map on her phone. It was, indeed, the street they had for Sam Gooding—West Great River Road. She flopped her hands against her sides. "Well, that figures."

A smattering of pedestrians weaved in between the girls as they stood on the sidewalk staring at the pharmacy.

"Now what?" Celeste asked.

"I should've known it was too good to be true," Morgan said. "Maybe there is a clue here, though."

Fiona took the alexandrite stone out of her pocket and aimed it toward the pharmacy. It didn't glow. She turned a full circle with it but it didn't indicate anything.

"Maybe it doesn't work anymore or maybe the clue really has nothing to do with Sam's house. He may have hidden it somewhere else," Celeste suggested.

"True." Morgan's eyes narrowed at something past Celeste's shoulder. "Hey, isn't that the museum guy? Henry?"

Jolene saw the curator from the Ephemera Museum standing on the corner. His eyes lit with recognition as he notice Jolene and her sisters.

"Hi, there. Remember us?" Fiona waved to Henry.

"Yes, yes, you were the ladies at the Museum yesterday, right?" Henry shuffled toward them, chuckling. "I never forget a pretty face, much less four of them."

"What brings you here?" Jolene figured he was probably going into the pharmacy for medicine.

"Just taking my morning constitutional. I try to get two walks in every day when the museum is not busy."

"Oh, that's right. I remember you said that yesterday," Morgan said.

"What brings you ladies here? Filling a prescription?" Henry nodded toward the pharmacy.

"Oh, no. We were just doing some research."

Henry pursed his lips. "You mean on the fellow you were asking about yesterday? Sam Gooding?"

Fiona nodded toward the building. "Yeah, we think we discovered where his house used to be. Now it's a pretty modern-looking pharmacy."

"That's the trouble. A lot of the old places were torn down to make way for progress." Henry cast a glance at the pharmacy and shook his head. "Well, I best be going. Can't stay away from the museum for too long. You ladies have a nice day."

"It makes perfect sense that his house wouldn't still be standing after three hundred years. But this is likely the location where his house *was*." Morgan looked down the street, her face a mixture of thoughtful concern.

Jolene recognized that Morgan was having a feeling of intuition and she wasn't surprised. She, herself, felt an energy shift. "You're getting one of your gut feelings, aren't you? I feel something, too. That niggling feeling that were being followed or watched."

"Exactly," Morgan said. "Do you sense another paranormal?"

"I'm not sure, but we better be prepared." Jolene's fist curled around the black obsidian amulet that hung at her neck.

Fiona had made each of them a similar amulet, specifically to help ward off negative energy that might be directed at them during a paranormal attack.

"Where is it?" Celeste's eyes darted around the area.

Jolene felt bad for her sister. Celeste didn't have the intuition that Morgan and Jolene did, and therefore had no idea which direction the threat was coming from. It was like going into a fight blind.

"It seems like it's over here." Jolene followed her instincts, heading west on the street toward a cluster of buildings. "I think there's something—"

"*Meow*!"

Two cats shot out from behind the buildings —the black cat they kept seeing, followed by a friend—a pure white cat.

"Is that Belladonna?" Celeste asked.

Jolene didn't stop to answer the question. She took off after the two cats. If it *was* Belladonna, she didn't want her wandering the streets.

The cats turned down a narrow alley. Jolene followed at full speed. She thought she heard a high-pitched cackle as she careened around the corner and then promptly tripped over a big, black cast-iron pot. She flew through the air and landed face first on the pavement.

Her sisters appeared at the mouth of the alley in time to see her land sprawled out on her stomach.

"Is that a cauldron?" Fiona asked incredulously.

"Looks like it." Jolene pushed to her feet and inspected her stinging palms.

"Are you okay?" Celeste asked.

"Fine. Did you see where they went?"

The sisters looked down the alley. It was empty except for three rusty blue dumpsters. There was an acrid smell of garbage.

"They could be anywhere." Celeste looked behind one of the dumpsters. "Do you think that was Belladonna? How did she get out?

"How does she ever get out?" Jolene asked. "This wouldn't be the first time she's suddenly appeared somewhere."

"I hope she's not rummaging in the dumpsters. It's not like we don't feed her plenty." Fiona gingerly picked up the lid of one of the dumpsters and peered inside.

"That's for sure." Jolene looked into the pot she tripped over. It had residue of a green liquid inside. "I wonder what this is doing here."

Fiona took out the gemstone and aimed at the pot. "Well, it's not a clue."

"Probably from the *Witches Brew*." Morgan pointed to a sign on one of the doors. "Looks like this is the back alley for that restaurant."

"Maybe they have breakfast," Fiona said hopefully. "We should check them out."

The cauldron *did* belong to the *Witches Brew* restaurant. Jolene was relieved to see that it was a promotional gimmick to have it in the alley. Not that she'd believed it was an actual witch's cauldron, but given the preponderance of black cats, the flying broomsticks and the cackle she thought she'd heard, she was almost starting to believe in witches. Especially after Mateo's mysterious words the evening before.

It turned out that the restaurant served up a pretty good breakfast and the girls ate hungrily, except for Celeste, who just had an herbal tea. They ordered lox minus the bagel and cream cheese for Belladonna, hoping the treat would stave off any unpleasant repercussions the cat might be conjuring up to punish them for keeping her locked in the hotel room, though Jolene wasn't totally convinced she hadn't gotten out and was running around Salem with the fluffy black cat.

They finished breakfast and headed back out onto the street.

"Where to next?" Fiona craned her neck, inspecting the other storefronts on the street. "There's no ice cream shop here."

"Forget about ice cream," Morgan said. "We need to get back to the hotel and dig a little deeper on Sam Gooding."

"Yeah, *and* make sure our cat hasn't done anything crazy," Celeste added.

Chapter 15

The closer they got to the hotel, the more jumpy Jolene became. She sensed something wasn't right. Or maybe she was just reacting to Morgan's nervous energy. Although Morgan was trying to act nonchalant, Jolene could see she was on alert, her eyes constantly darting about as they walked. Jolene knew Morgan's intuition was telling her to be cautious.

Jolene spent the time *not* thinking about Mateo. Well, not hardly. He hadn't called or texted her. She shouldn't be surprised. He often just disappeared without even saying goodbye. It was his modus operandi. She wondered if he was off with the long-haired beauty she'd seen him with. Did he kiss *her* after their meal, too?

Thoughts of Matco were crowded out of her mind by a surge of energy as they approached the door to their hotel room.

Morgan felt it, too, and shot her arms out to stop Fiona and Celeste from entering. "Something's not right," Morgan whispered.

Celeste put the to-go bag with Belladonna's lox on the floor and the sisters dialed up their energy levels, each of them knowing they might need to call on the full power of their gifts if they were attacked.

Morgan slipped the key card into the lock quietly.

Click.

She shoved the door open and the four of them sprang inside, clutching their obsidian amulets and summoning all their energy, ready to defend themselves against whoever was waiting inside.

"*Meow*!" Belladonna leaped down from the counter and leisurely trotted over to them.

The sisters carefully checked each room, but Jolene knew they wouldn't find anyone. Belladonna would never have been so lackadaisical if an intruder was in there.

But someone *had* been in there. Jolene could see the energy trail. "Someone was here." Jolene pointed at the floor as if her sisters could see the fading trail of brown energy.

"Did they take something? Where did they go?" Fiona asked.

But the energy trail traipsed all over the hotel suite and was quickly fading. "It looks like they went everywhere."

"That's odd. I wouldn't think Belladonna would let anyone in here," Celeste said.

Jolene remembered the white and black cats she'd chased down the alleyway. "Maybe Belladonna wasn't here."

At first glance, it didn't look like anything had been taken or disturbed, but Jolene called upon her photographic memory to remember how the hotel room had looked when they'd left. She could tell that the papers that had been on the desk had been moved carefully and put back. "Someone did look through our things. It's subtly different. It's almost as if they didn't want us to know they were here."

"Was it a paranormal?" Fiona asked.

"Possibly, but not the same energy trail that I saw at Amity Jones' house," Jolene said.

"Maybe we have more than one paranormal on our trail," Celeste suggested.

"*Mew!*" Belladonna's tail and ears went up and she trotted over to the door sniffing underneath.

"Someone's out in the hall," Morgan whispered as she tiptoed over to the door.

Jolene, her energy still at full power, sensed it, too.

Celeste got on one side of the door and the other three lined up on the other side. They tensed, ready to attack whoever was out there. Was it the person who had broken in earlier?

Morgan gave the nod and Celeste jerked open the door.

Jolene's heart crunched when she saw who was standing outside. It was Mateo, and he wasn't alone. Standing next to him—very closely—was the dark-haired beauty.

Morgan relaxed. "Oh, it's just you."

"It's good to see you, too." Mateo smiled through his sarcastic reply, his eyes seeking out Jolene.

She'd crossed to the other side of the room in order to be as far away from him as possible. Her chest constricted when their eyes met, and she quickly looked away, then leaned a slim hip against the desk and crossed her arms. The nerve of him, bringing his gorgeous girlfriend here after trying to kiss her!

Morgan opened the door wide. "Come on in."

"What's going on? I sense worry," Mateo said.

"Someone was in our room," Fiona answered.

"Is anything missing?"

"We don't think so. At least we haven't found anything missing, yet."

Mateo glanced around the room, frowning. "It's a good thing we came, then. We debated telling you this but ... well, Cassiopeia felt very strongly that you might need to know."

Jolene noticed Morgan's eyes narrow at the woman, Cassiopeia. Darn right she should glare at her, Jolene thought, though it was more appropriate that *Mateo* be the recipient of Morgan's steely gaze. More likely, Morgan should be feeling sorry for Cassiopeia. The woman probably had no idea what she was getting herself into with Mateo.

"Hey, aren't you the woman from the mystical shop in Freeport?" Fiona asked.

Jolene's suspicion meter pegged into the red. That was a strange coincidence—the woman who was the source of this whole thing showing up with Mateo?

Mateo nodded. "She is. This is Cassiopeia Ortiz. My sister."

"Sister?" Morgan said. "I didn't know you had one."

Mateo grinned. "There are a lot of things you don't know about me."

Morgan shot an arched-brow look at Jolene.

Jolene knew exactly what that look meant. It was Morgan's way of saying 'see, you were worrying about Mateo with another woman for nothing'. But Jolene was not placated. She still had unsettled feelings about Mateo. Sure, he wasn't hanging out with a beautiful woman—or at least not this beautiful woman—but he still hadn't called after their date. She didn't know why it bothered her so much. She wasn't in the market for a steady boyfriend, especially not one who disappeared for months on end like Mateo was apt to do.

"*Meowurrr!*" Belladonna wound a figure eight around Cassiopeia's ankles, earning a scratch behind the ears.

Traitor. Jolene glared at the cat. Belladonna might take to Cassiopeia right off the bat, but Jolene certainly wasn't going to, even if she was Mateo's sister. Jolene was just in that kind of mood at the moment.

Belladonna butted her head against Cassiopeia's hand, then trotted over to the other side of the room, near the doorway to their bedrooms.

"*Merowl!*"

"What's she up to?" Mateo asked.

"Nothing. She's been acting strange today. I think she's mad that we went out to breakfast," Celeste answered.

"I'm just glad she didn't get out," Morgan laughed. "We thought we saw her outside and if she was trotting around the halls of the hotel, we would be in a lot of trouble with the owner."

"Yeah, we've already been warned a couple of times about keeping her in her crate. I know what will settle her down, though." Jolene went back out into the hall to get the bag with the lox that they'd left there. Brushing past Mateo, she ignored the warm rush of electricity that jolted through her when their arms touched. She concentrated on ignoring Mateo while she put the lox in Belladonna food dish.

Her sisters brought Mateo and Cassiopeia up to speed on their research into Sam Gooding and how they suspected he had left a clue as to where the scrying ball was hidden.

Belladonna purred and butted her head against Jolene as if in a show of solidarity against Mateo, Jolene imagined. She took comfort in petting Belladonna's silky fur, running her fingers from the tips of her ears all the way down her body to the tip of her tail, which she noticed was tinged with green... just like the green that was in the cauldron.

Had Belladonna actually been out in that alley? That would explain why someone had been able to break in their room and escape relatively unscathed. Jolene had seen Belladonna scratch their 'enemies' up pretty bad and, although she didn't actually know the intruder was unscathed,

Belladonna would be more riled up now if she'd been here when someone had broken in.

"So, what is so important?" Morgan asked once they were all settled on the sofa and chairs.

"We can speak freely." Mateo nodded toward his sister. "Like me, Cassiopeia is a paranormal. Well, she's actually more than a paranormal. She has additional powers and we think it might be time that you girls discovered yours."

"Additional powers?" Jolene said. "Like what?"

Cassiopeia spoke, her voice deep and melodic, "There's much more to your powers than you ladies know."

"We've been working on developing them. Just this past year I made a major breakthrough with mine." Fiona pulled her hand from her pocket and opened her clenched fist, showing a handful of pebbles that glowed like lava.

"I know," Cassiopeia said. "But what I'm talking about is something on another level."

"Another level? What do you mean?" Morgan asked. "Is there something that will make us even more powerful?"

Mateo and Cassiopeia exchanged a knowing glance. "Yes, you will become more powerful. This new level could give you an edge over mere paranormals."

"*Mere* paranormals? You mean there are different kinds of paranormals?" Morgan asked.

"Yes."

Morgan leaned forward, her elbows on her thighs. "Okay, you have my interest. What is this 'new level' you're talking about?"

"The ability to use spells and charms with your paranormal gifts," Cassiopeia said.

Jolene snorted. "Spells and charms? You mean like witches?"

"Yeah, we don't believe in that stuff." Morgan looked around at her sisters. "Do we?"

"No." Fiona shook her head. "It's taken us a while to come to terms with our paranormal abilities but we're comfortable with those now. We realize we're different from other people. More sensitive to energy. But witches? We're not witches."

"Yeah, I don't think there really are such things as witches. Maybe what you think are witches are just really powerful paranormals," Morgan suggested.

"Or maybe you guys have been hanging around in Salem too much," Jolene added.

Cassiopeia sighed and turned to Mateo. "Maybe you were right, they're not ready."

"They have to be ready. We need to find the crystal ball soon before it falls into the wrong hands. Others are looking." Mateo turned serious. "Look, you guys, you don't have to believe in this stuff right now, but what harm would it do to memorize one of the spells? Just in case you need it."

Morgan shrugged. "I guess it can't hurt and if it keeps you guys from pestering us about it then let's just do it."

"Well, you can't 'just do it'," Cassiopeia said. "The spell can work for anything you want. It has unlimited power. But it needs to be said with heartfelt intent in order for it to work."

"What does that mean?" Jolene asked.

"When you say it, you have to really mean it," Mateo answered.

"What is this spell, anyway?" Morgan asked. "Maybe you could just tell us what it is and then if we need to use it we'll muster up some heartfelt intent."

Cassiopeia rolled her eyes and looked at Mateo. "I think they will need a guide. Maybe I should stick around."

"Guide?" Fiona asked.

"Someone more experienced with spells. To help boost the intent. Until you guys learn how." Mateo turned to Cassiopeia. "I'll be with them. Tell them the words so at least they'll be armed."

Cassiopeia sighed. "Fine, but you must be very careful how you use this. These words are powerful:

By Water, Earth, Air and Fire,
I ask thee now grant my desire,
Harming none I now decree
This charm is done, so mote it be."

"Meow!"

"See, even Belladonna knows how important the words are," Mateo pointed out amidst laughter from everyone.

"Well, I think I've done what I came for and now I will wish you ladies good luck. I need to get back to Freeport," Cassiopeia said.

Mateo got up from the sofa. "I'll walk you out, Sis." He looked back at them, his eyes seeking out Jolene who pretended like she was busy shuffling papers at the desk. "I hardly ever get time to spend with my little sister. You know how it is."

"Sure, don't worry about us." Morgan followed them to the door and shut it behind them.

"Well, that was interesting," Fiona said.

"Yeah. I didn't know he had a sister," Celeste added.

"I meant about the spell," Fiona said.

"What you think, Jolene?" Morgan asked.

Jolene shrugged. "I doubt a spell is going to help us and I don't think we need one. We're pretty powerful now, especially since Fiona has mastered using those pebbles as weapons."

"Actually, I was talking about Cassiopeia being Mateo's sister," Morgan smirked. "That's the one you keep seeing him with, isn't it? The one you're jealous of?"

Jolene bristled. "I'm not jealous. I have no claim on Mateo. In fact, I'm not even looking for a boyfriend. He can go off to wherever he goes and we'll get along perfectly fine without his help."

"You can argue that until you're blue in the face. None of us believe you." Fiona chuckled. "I think we should get back on track trying to figure out where Sam Gooding hid that crystal ball." Fiona stood up and walked to her room. "I'll get my phone and see if I can help Google information. I left it on the charger."

"I'm more concerned about the person who was in here. Why was he here and what did he want?" Celeste asked.

"*Merow!*" Belladonna followed Fiona into her room.

"We've felt that we've been followed all along," Morgan said. "We know there are others looking for the scrying ball. I'm sure they found out we were staying here and decided to break in and see what we have on it."

"Oh, no!" Fiona shouted in her bedroom.

"*Mepow*!"

Fiona appeared in the doorway her face white as a sheet. "My crystals are missing. Someone has stolen them!"

Chapter 16

"Your crystals?" Morgan's asked with concern.

"Yes, the ones from Mariah Blackmoore."

Fiona referred to a cache of powerful crystals the sisters had found in the attic of their home. Hidden in a burlap bag with the initials MB on it, they assumed the crystals had once belonged to their ancestor, Mariah Blackmoore.

"It was probably whoever killed Nancy," Jolene decided. The killer took Opal's book so he would have known there was a crystal or gemstone that would lead him to the scrying ball. He must have thought it was in with the others." She frowned at the floor. "Or not. The energy trail is different from the one I saw at Amity Jones' house."

Fiona pulled the alexandrite gemstone out of her pocket and held it up. "Well, whoever it was didn't get it."

"But whoever it was knows about the link between the stone and the scrying ball," Celeste pointed out.

"And possibly that we followed the relic trail with the help of a gemstone or crystal from Amity Jones' collection," Morgan added.

"Yeah, gee, who do we know that knows about crystals and also knows that we're looking for the same thing Amity Jones was?" Jolene asked sarcastically.

"Opal Mines." Morgan bolted to the door. "We better go pay her a visit."

It didn't take long to get to Opal's shop. Ten minutes later, they were inside Opal's shop, alone, no Opal Mines in sight.

Morgan called out, "Opal, are you out back!"

No one answered. Just the faint hoot of an owl sounded out on the street.

"This is weird. She wouldn't just go out and leave the place unlocked, would she?" Celeste asked.

"Maybe that's what she does when she's breaking into people's hotel rooms," Jolene said.

Morgan shook her head. "No. Something's not right."

Jolene felt it, too. The crystal balls in the shop had on an eerie glow. She looked into one of the display cases and saw an image in one of the crystal orbs: a pair of feet—toes up.

"Uh-oh."

"What?" Morgan looked over Jolene's shoulder into the display case.

But the image was gone. It had been there long enough, though, for Jolene to determine the floor looked exactly like the one they were now standing on. She turned around and surveyed the room. There was a doorway to the back. A storage room? She made her way over and pulled open the door, her heart twisting when she saw Opal's body on the floor. She recognized the shoes that she'd seen in the crystal ball.

"Oh, no!" Fiona pushed Jolene out of the way and ran to the body. She dug the carnelian stones out of her pocket, but once again she was too late. Opal was beyond help. "She's dead! And not by natural causes." Fiona pointed to the purple marks on Opal's neck.

"Do you think she was killed by a paranormal? The same person who killed Nancy?" Celeste asked.

"And possibly Amity," Morgan reminded them.

Jolene turned up her energy awareness and searched the room for an energy trail, but everything was fuzzy. "I think I see a little bit of an energy trail right here in the storeroom. The same one I saw at Amity's house. But it's fuzzy. I think

146

the crystal balls are messing with it, so I can't say that it is the same trail."

Morgan glanced around the store. "That makes sense. I felt like the crystals diminished my abilities when we were here before."

Fiona stood up. "Clearly Opal is messed up in this somehow, but if she stole our crystals, I wonder if they're here."

They looked around the storeroom, but didn't see the burlap bag.

"Maybe whoever killed her took them," Jolene suggested.

"That could bc," Fiona said.

"Yes, but who is it … and what are they going to do next?" Morgan asked.

"There are a lot of unanswered questions." Celeste turned thoughtful. "Maybe we should use that spell."

Jolene laughed. "You're joking, right? That spell isn't going to help us. Don't you think Mom would have said something to us if spells could help with our gifts?"

Celeste inclined her head. "You have a point. Mom would've let us know. She's been dealing with her powers a lot longer and knows everything about them. Though she did seem receptive to the idea that witches existed."

"Yeah, but she never said anything about spells. Besides we can figure this out on our own," Morgan said.

"Unfortunately, now we're going to have to call Officer Unpleasant and tell him we found another body," Fiona added.

"Let's not tell him about the break in, though," Morgan said as she pulled out her phone. "I'm not sure we can trust him, or anyone we've met in Salem."

While they waited for the police to show up, Jolene wandered around the shop, noting the various types of crystal balls. They came in various shapes, sizes and clarity. She peered into each one, but did not see another vision.

A movement outside caught Jolene's eye. An energy shiver ran up her spine. She looked across the street, her eyes locking with a pair of dark brown ones set wide in a pale face. The face belonged to a woman wearing a long black flowing cape similar to the one she kept seeing bits and pieces of wherever she went.

She sidled over to Morgan and whispered, "I think that woman is the person who's been following us."

Morgan's eyes flicked out onto the street. "I knew someone was following us! Should we chase her?"

Jolene was already sprinting for the door. As soon as she got to the street, the woman pivoted and took off like a racehorse. Jolene ran after her, but the woman was too fast.

The streets were old and narrow, with twists and turns, and the cloaked woman had an advantage. She knew how to navigate the maze of side streets as she turned down one street and then another.

Rounding a corner, Jolene skidded to a stop. The woman was gone, as if she'd simply disappeared into thin air.

When Jolenc got back to Opal's shop, Detective Peterson was there with his entourage who were already dusting for fingerprints and putting out little yellow placards where they found something of interest. Peterson was scowling at her sisters.

"Should I be suspicious that you ladies found another dead body?" Peterson turned as Jolene entered the shop. "And where were you?"

"Someone was outside staring into the shop." Jolene bent over, her hands on her knees trying to catch her breath. "She looked suspicious, so I gave chase. Maybe you should be looking for her instead of questioning us. She looked like the person we saw in the woods by Amity Jones' cottage."

Peterson frowned. "And just what did this suspicious woman look like?"

"Long dark hair, brown eyes, pale face and she was wearing a long black top that flowed out behind her."

"Like a witch's cape?" The corners of Peterson's mouth ticked up in amusement.

Jolene shrugged. "Yeah, I guess so."

"And where did she go?"

Jolene glanced back out toward the street. "Well, I couldn't really follow her. She was fast and she went off that way down the street but then she kind of ... disappeared and I lost her trail."

"Disappeared? Or maybe she flew off on her broomstick." Peterson said.

"I'm just telling you I saw someone acting suspiciously."

Peterson sighed and scrubbed his hand across his face. "Sure, I get that. But how many people do you think there are who look like a witch here in Salem?"

"I get your point," Morgan said. "But if we were the killers, do you really think we would keep calling you about finding the bodies?"

Peterson's eyes narrowed. "Probably not. But you have to admit, it is a little suspicious that you keep finding them. It can't be a coincidence. Just what is it that you're after, anyway?"

"Research project," Jolene said innocently.

"Uh-huh. So that's why you were at Amity Jones' cottage and why you're now here in the crystal ball shop."

Fiona waved her hands to indicate the shop, making the crystals throb and Peterson's eyes narrow in surprise. "I have my own crystal shop at home. I create healing jewelry. We figured while we were here we'd connect with others in the business. Check out their wares and so on."

"So you're just unlucky and everyone you visit ends up dead?" Peterson asked.

Fiona shrugged. "Very unlucky."

Peterson nodded. "Okay, so then why were you skulking around the Rebecca Nurse house after hours?"

"As we told you before, that was one of the tourist attractions that we planned to visit while we were in town," Jolene answered.

"Surely, that's not out of the ordinary?" Morgan added.

"Not at all." Peterson turned to Jolene. "And what about your research project?"

"Huh?"

"You said you were researching something … is that for a university class or are you some kind of research scientist?"

"University," Jolene said.

"And what's that about?" Peterson persisted.

"Sam Gooding. One of the people involved in the witch trials."

Peterson's brow creased. "I don't think I've heard of him. I've become somewhat of an expert on this Salem witch business. That's why this case has me so bothered. There are some elements that are ... well, just let me say otherworldly."

Fiona arched a brow. "Oh, really? Like what?"

Peterson shifted his position and lowered his voice. "Well, I can't really say much. I don't really believe in witchcraft and all that, but Amity Jones was rumored to be involved with the paranormal, as was Opal. And now you're saying you saw a witch outside looking into the shop. There's something funny going on here. Something dangerous. You ladies might be smart to stick to the more prominent tourist sites while you're in town."

Jolene thought he almost sounded sincere. Was he actually concerned for their safety? Is that why he was asking so many questions? She amped up her energy to try to read his aura. She'd be able to tell by the color if he was actually trying to help them or if he was pulling a fast one. But the crystal balls in the shop interfered with her gift and she couldn't get a good reading.

"I think we've been to the most interesting museums in Salem," Celeste said.

"Yeah, it's too bad that most of the old houses and buildings are gone, replaced by modern buildings," Fiona added.

"It is a shame a lot of the old buildings were lost," Peterson agreed. "But there are still quite a few buildings left standing. People get confused because Salem Village, where the witch trials took place, is not the same geographical location as modern day Salem. And, of course, not all the witches were from Salem, anyway. So there are plenty of historical places left standing if you know where to look."

"Wait, you mean the streets listed in the old records that have to do with the witch trials wouldn't necessarily correlate to streets here in Salem?" Morgan asked.

"Right," Peterson nodded. "Most of them would be over in Danvers. That's where the village was in 1692. You know, where I caught you at the Rebecca Nurse house."

A flash of hope coursed through Jolene. Maybe Sam Gooding's house really did still stand, just not in the location they thought it was.

" Well, if you're done with us ..." Jolene gestured toward the door.

"Yeah I'm done with you. Remember what I said, though. And ladies ..."

"Yes?" Jolene turned back to him as she pushed the door open.

"Don't let me catch you bending over another dead body."

Chapter 17

The sisters made it back to their hotel in record time.

"I can't believe we didn't think of that." Morgan tapped the map. "The original map was here the whole time."

Fiona looked at the map over her sister's shoulder. "Yeah, all we had to do was look at the streets and realize they didn't match up with present-day Salem."

"*Meow!*"

"That's why Belladonna kept pushing the map off the desk the other day." Jolene squinted at the small map. "But I don't see any Great River Road here."

"Let me see" Fiona pulled a small round loupe used for magnifying gemstones out of her pocket and bent over the paper, meticulously going over every line. She sighed and straightened. "She's right. It's not on there."

"There's a lot of blank area on the map. Maybe all the streets aren't filled in," Celeste suggested.

"Good thinking." Jolene opened her laptop and her fingers flew over the keyboard.

Morgan, Fiona and Celeste watched with rapt attention. Even Belladonna sat quietly on the side of the desk, her tail twitching back and forth in time with Jolene's key tapping.

"There's nothing. Nothing about a Great River Road in Salem Village *or* in Danvers," Jolene said after a few minutes. "The street names could have changed over the years, though. If that happened hundreds of years ago, I doubt there would be a record online."

"So, we need an older source of information. Older than the Internet," Morgan said.

Jolene flattened her palms on the desk and pushed herself out of the chair. "That's right, and we know exactly where to get that, don't we?"

Ten minutes later they were piling out of the SUV in front of the Ephemera Museum. Henry was behind the desk, his eyebrows barely lifting as the four of them entered the alcove of the musty museum.

"You ladies are getting to be regulars." His eyes sparkled.

"We have some more research to do," Jolene said. "We have a map of old Salem Village, but we don't think all the streets are marked on it. Do you have anything that might list more streets?"

Henry thought a minute and then nodded. "Yep. I do. Is this related to the Sam Gooding fellow you were asking about? I thought his house was where that pharmacy is now."

"We made the mistake of thinking the address was in Salem when it's really in Danvers. That's where Salem Village *was*. But Danvers doesn't have any such street and the old map doesn't show where it is, so we're having a hard time correlating it to a modern street."

Henry shuffled into the back then came out a few seconds later with a cardboard tube. He pried the plastic end off the tube and slid a map out. He unfurled on top of a glass case. The map was similar to the 1692 Salem map the girls had but much more detailed.

"What was the street name?" he asked as they all bent over the map.

"West Great River Road." Morgan stabbed her finger at the map. "Here it is, right here!"

"Next to this river. What is this river?" Jolene asked, running her finger along the blue line that ran parallel to the road.

"Ah, yes. That makes sense," Henry said. "That's the Ipswich River now. Back then they called it the Great River. But I don't think you want that road."

Jolene's brows tucked together. "Why not? It says right there Great River Road."

"You girls said *West* Great River. That road there is east of the river. But this road ..." Henry pointed at a thin line on the west side of the river. "This is West Great River. I remember it now. It's an old dirt road. The whole area there dates back to the 1600s. There were houses there at one time. In fact, you can still see the cellar holes. There's no record of what happened to those houses and the land has gone wild. It's never been developed. Some say it's haunted." Henry chuckled, then turned serious. "Maybe you ladies had better not venture out there. Could be trouble."

"We're not afraid of trouble." Jolene thought the area sounded perfect, especially if it was haunted. Celeste might see a ghost who'd tell them where to find the scrying ball. It was possible the area had never been developed because there was some paranormal energy protecting the crystal ball. She had a feeling they were finally on the right track.

***

Henry wasn't kidding when he said the area had never been developed. They drove into the woods as far as they could and then got out of the

SUV. If there had been houses there at one time, Jolene could see no sign of them. The area was overgrown with shrubs and trees. Only a slightly visible path meandered among the pines, oaks and shrubs. The distant trickle of the river told them they were on the right trail.

The further they walked, the more out of sorts Jolene felt.

"Are you sure this is the right place?" Morgan asked.

Fiona checked the map she held in her hand. After leaving the Ephemera Museum, they'd compared satellite photos to the photograph they'd taken of the 1692 paper map and discovered a path that should lead to the general area of Sam Gooding's house. "According to our research, it is. Why do you ask?"

"I feel a little funny. I think my intuition is kicking in and if I'm reading it correctly this is not the direction we should be heading." Morgan glanced over her shoulder. "Also, I think someone is following us."

The girls turned around, but no one was there.

"Do you think it's the detective?" Celeste asked. "I sure hope we don't find a body out here. I don't think he'll be as nice to us if we come up with a third one."

"I don't think it's him," Morgan said. "Besides, we're not in Salem so, if we do find a body, it won't be Peterson that comes to investigate."

"That didn't stop him before. He followed us to the Rebecca Nurse house," Fiona pointed out.

"True, but I don't think he's following us," Morgan said. "He actually seemed almost helpful and friendly at Opal's."

"Yeah, he did, didn't he? Maybe he really is just concerned about our welfare," Celeste said.

"And anyway, *why* would he follow us?" Fiona asked. "Unless you think Peterson's looking for the scrying ball, too."

The hairs on Jolene's neck prickled. Maybe they should take Morgan's feelings seriously. "Well, *someone* is looking for the scrying ball, and they broke into our room and stole the crystals to help their effort. By now they've figured out the alexandrite wasn't there, so it makes sense whoever it is would be following us to take the keystone from us."

Fiona shook her head. "I doubt that was Peterson. How could he kill Opal and then be back at the police station in time to respond to the call? Or our call about Nancy, for that matter?"

"We don't know exactly when Opal or Nancy died," Morgan pointed out.

"Good point," Fiona said. "I would have pegged Opal for the one following us and the one who broke in, but now that she's dead I'm not so sure. Still, it could be anyone. Peterson might just be trying to keep us out of trouble."

"That's usually Mateo's job," Jolene said and then wondered why saying his name caused her heart to beat faster. "But it looks like he's disappeared, as usual."

Swoosh.

Jolene whipped around. There was nothing behind them but trees. "Did you hear that?"

"Yes. A funny sound. Behind us, right?" Morgan answered.

"I heard it, too." Fiona's hand strayed to her pocket where she kept her stones. "Is the forest getting darker?"

"It's denser here and I think the sun has gone behind clouds, but yes, it does seem darker." Jolene focused on following the barely visible path which now seemed much harder to follow. She turned to Celeste. "Any sign of ghosts? We sure could use one to tell us what's going on or direct us to the right place."

"Sorry, I don't see even a quiver of ectoplasmic goo." Celeste yawned.

Jolene realized she was very tired, too. She looked around at her sisters, whose previous energetic enthusiasm seemed to be draining.

Swoosh!

Jolene whipped her head in the direction of the odd sound. A pile of leaves swirled up from the ground and the air shimmered.

"Over there!" Fiona yelled.

Jolene whirled around to see her sister pointing at something in the opposite direction. "What is it?" Jolene asked.

"I'm not sure," Fiona said. "It was murky. But I thought I saw something in a black cape."

"Like the witch Jolene saw at Opal's? Maybe she's the one who's been following us," Celeste said.

"And if it is her, I think she's a paranormal. I'm getting a strange energy vibe. There's someone out here and I think they might have a geode." A chill ran up Jolene's spine. Certain geodes could be bad news for her and her sisters. They drained all their energy and knocked them unconscious. Normally, though, the enemy would have to be standing right in front of them, holding the geode toward them. But no one was in front of them.

Morgan spun around. "I feel it, too. It feels like the energy is being drained right out of me. But I don't see anybody. And this feels different, somehow."

"It does. Maybe that's what Henry meant when he said the place was haunted," Celeste said.

"Should we keep going?" Fiona asked.

"We should if we want to find the house, or where it was." Morgan scanned the forest. "I don't see anything, though."

The wind picked up, rustling through the trees noisily. Jolene noticed that the birds, squirrels and chipmunks that had been happily skittering around the forest when they'd started out, were nowhere to be seen now. Her nerves were frazzled. She felt both jumpy and tired at the same time. The ringing in her ears grew louder with each step she took. The air shimmered, almost as if she were looking through a waterfall.

"I don't feel so good." Celeste passed her hand over her brow.

"Neither do I," Fiona said.

"Me, either. What's causing it?" Morgan asked.

"I don't know. Let's stop and rest." But Jolene couldn't stop. It was as if she was being pulled by some magnetic force deeper into the woods, her feet pressing one in front of the other, seemingly of their own volition.

"Oh, no, it's a vortex!" Morgan yelled as the sisters tried to resist the pull.

"What?" Fiona slid in the damp leaves as she tried to stop from moving forward.

"An energy hole, like a whirlpool but in the air. It's pulling us toward that rock." Morgan indicated a gigantic rock fifty feet away. "This area has had some sort of energy infusion. The closer we get, the stronger the pull is—we can't get away!"

Jolene tried to resist, but the more she tried to turn back, the more she was pulled towards the rock. It was like being in quicksand.

"Hehehehehehe." A deafening cackle split the air, coming from all sides, surrounding them.

And then Jolene saw her, the black-caped witch standing in between two white birch trees. But there wasn't just *one* of her. There were two. No ... four ... no, six. She was multiplying in front of Jolene's eyes. And then she thrust out her hand, her impossibly long fingernails clawing their way toward Jolene.

"Grab my hand. It's the only way to get out."

Jolene looked at her sisters, panic spreading in her chest. "Do you see her? Did you hear that?"

"Yes." Morgan had to yell over the sound of static that was whipping through the air as a cold wind rose up pushing the sisters further toward the rock.

Jolene tried to inch away, but it was like walking against the tide. Her feet were moving away from the rock but she was still going toward it.

"Is it her doing this?" Celeste pressed her hands over her ears.

"It must be. No one else is here."

"I'm here to *help* you. Take my hand. It's the only way you'll get out." The witch's voice was very far away but had a soothing, compelling tone.

Jolene had a desperate urge to take the woman's hand.

"Should we trust her?" Fiona uncurled her fist to reveal five red glowing pebbles. "I can try these rocks."

"And then what? We'll be stuck in here." Morgan screwed up her face, then grabbed onto a pine tree as a strong gust pushed the girls further toward the rock. "We're losing ground. I have a feeling ... an intuition that she may really be the only way out."

Jolene's hair whipped around her face, the wind dried out her eyes, the sound of static—and her own heartbeat—pounded in her ears. She'd always trusted Morgan's intuition before and it had never steered them wrong.

Jolene took a deep breath and reached out toward the witch.

Chapter 18

A dry, rough hand latched onto Jolene with a vise-like grip. She felt the stinging bite of razor sharp claws on her palm as she was yanked away from the rock with a force that was otherworldly.

Her lungs tightened, squeezing all the air out. She couldn't catch her breath, her chest compressing smaller and smaller like a witch being pressed to death with heavy stones. The rush of her blood in her ears drowned everything out except for the screams of her sisters.

The air suddenly cleared, as if by magic.

Jolene sucked in a breath as she staggered to the ground between two trees. The hand, still holding hers, now felt warm and soft. Inviting. Welcoming. She rolled onto her knees, choking and sputtering. Beside her, Morgan, Fiona and Celeste were doing the same.

In front of them stood the witch, hands on hips, narrowed eyes assessing them. Jolene noticed that she wasn't wearing a cloak at all. The black material was a long, loose tunic, the knee-length feathered edges flapping in the breeze.

"What the heck did you do to us?" Morgan sputtered.

"Me? I saved you from ..." The witch turned and waved at the big rock. "That."

Jolene pushed herself up to her feet. She glanced from the witch to the rock that, impossible though it seemed, was now a good two hundred feet away. "What *is* that ... and *who* are you?"

"*That* is an energy vortex. It's a good thing I was here because you were only seconds from being swallowed up into that thing." The witch looked at the rock and shivered.

Morgan got to her feet beside Jolene. "And just why *were* you here? Have you been following us?"

"Yeah. It's about time you people noticed. Who do you think was protecting you all this time?"

Fiona picked pine needles out of her hair. "Protecting us? From what?"

"Bad energy. Paranormals. You guys can't be stupid enough to think that no one else is after the scrying ball."

Celeste's brows shot up. "You know about that. *Who* are you anyway?"

The witch shot her hand out. Jolene shook it, surprised to see it wasn't green and gnarled with long sharp fingernails. It was just a normal hand. "I'm Sarah Easty. I already know who you are."

"Sarah Easty?" Celeste brushed the leaves off the back of her black yoga pants. "But I thought you —"

"That's my ancestor. She was hanged on Gallows Hill for witchcraft. She's stuck over at the Nurse house, can't leave the tree, so I have to help her out. You talked to her ghost."

"Help her out?"

"She's sworn to protect the crystal ball as am I. She can't move on until it's in the right hands ... your hands," Sarah said. "I've been trying to make sure nothing happens to you guys before you find it."

"How do we know you're not trying to take the crystal ball for yourself?" Fiona asked.

"Seriously? If I was after it, do you think I would be running myself ragged to protect you?"

"How have you been protecting us?" Morgan asked. "I haven't seen you do any protecting. I think you've just been *following* us."

"Well, apparently you aren't very observant. You were followed by paranormals to Amity Jones' house the day you discovered Nancy's body. They were waiting outside with geodes. I had to put a newt charm on them. And then, the other day at the crystal ball shop I had just turned two burley bearded guys with energy guns into owls before you girls came bursting onto the scene."

"Dr. Bly's people," Celeste said. "They always seem to have beards for some reason. Wait, you turned them into owls?"

Sarah nodded. "I know, the poor owl community. I feel bad, but they'll assimilate quite nicely and, hopefully, learn some manners."

Fiona nodded. "They probably killed Opal."

Sarah nodded. "Possibly. But that isn't really important now. Helping you find the scrying ball is, but what in the world were you girls doing out *here*? Everyone in the paranormal community knows this place is cursed."

"Yeah, well, *we* didn't. We thought this was the location of Sam Gooding's house." Morgan looked around the area, then back at Sarah. "How do we know you're not just trying to throw us off track?"

Sarah shrugged. "I'm from Witches' Guild Number 785. We've been tasked with helping you ... I thought you guys knew that."

"Witches have guilds?" Celeste asked in amazement.

"Yep. We're organized, just like any other group. My leader, Cassiopeia Ortiz, entrusted me with this assignment."

"If you know Cassiopeia, then you must know Mateo," Morgan said.

"I do, indeed."

Jolene took a closer look at Sarah. Her brown eyes were flecked with gold and set wide on her heart-shaped face. Her flawless, alabaster skin was framed by dark hair, long and cut in layers. She found herself wondering how well Sarah knew Mateo, an unwanted flush of jealousy heating her cheeks.

"Why didn't Cassiopeia—or Mateo—come here themselves?" A hint of suspicion crept into Jolene's voice.

"Cassi is up in Freeport. She's regional and there's a problem ... well, you don't need to know our inner troubles." Sarah glanced behind her. "And Mateo is ... here."

Jolene looked around "He is? I don't see him."

"He's back at the car. He didn't want to get too close to the vortex. It gives him the creeps." Sarah gave Jolene a knowing look. "You know how guys are. They can't handle this kind of thing. Anyway speaking of that, it gives *me* the creeps too. Shall we go?"

Morgan studied Sarah for a minute, then gave a nod of approval. Apparently, her intuition told her Sarah was a friend. "Yeah. Let's go"

As they started down the trail, a black cat ran across the path in front of them.

"Hey, watch out!" Celeste yelled.

"Oh, don't worry about Raven. That whole thing about a black cat crossing your path being bad luck is just an old wives' tale," Sarah said.

"*Meow*." Raven peered at them from behind an oak tree.

"Is that your cat?" Fiona asked Sarah.

"Not really. It's more like I'm her human."

"Yeah, we know how that is." Jolene half expected to see Belladonna run across the path, too. In fact Raven looked just like the black cat she'd seen this morning and she was almost positive Belladonna had been with her.

As they trudged back along the path, Jolene's spirits sank. "Looks like our lead on Gooding's house was another dead end. Now what do we do?"

"I'm sorry I can't be much help on that. I'm just here to protect," Sarah said

They came to the end of the path and Jolene noticed a maroon Toyota Corolla parked behind their SUV.

"You drive a Toyota?" Morgan asked Sarah.

"Yes. What did you think, that I rode in on a broomstick? That's an old wives' tale, too." Sarah rolled her eyes. "You girls have a lot to learn about witches."

Jolene was about to enlighten Sarah as to how they didn't actually believe in witches when

173

she noticed someone leaning against the other side of the SUV. It was Mateo, wearing a black tee shirt that showed off just enough muscle, his long legs kicked out in front of him as he leaned on the hood. A smile bloomed when he noticed Jolene. Their eyes clicked.

Jolene's momentary stomach flutter was pierced by a stab of jealousy as Mateo's eyes skimmed past her and zeroed in on Sarah. She pushed away unkind thoughts. Sarah had saved them from the vortex and now Jolene *owed* her, so it wouldn't be right to feel animosity toward the woman.

"Nice job, Sarah. Thanks," Mateo said.

"No problem." Sarah opened the driver's side door of the Toyota. "You got it from here?"

Mateo nodded. "Yep."

As Sarah got into her car, Mateo turned his attention to the Blackmoore sisters. "You okay?" He came to stand beside Jolene and slipped his arm around her shoulders. "I've been looking all over for you."

Jolene slipped out from under his arm reluctantly. It felt good to be that close to him, but... He couldn't just almost kiss her and then run off with no phone call the next day, and expect to just pick up where he'd left off. "You have?" she said frostily. "You could've called."

"I did. And I texted you like five times. You never answered."

"What?" Jolene dug in her pocket for her phone.

Morgan, Celeste and Fiona clustered around the map, and tried not to look like they were eavesdropping.

Jolene frowned down at the phone. Dead battery.

Mateo took her hand, his eyes filled with concern. "Really, are you okay?"

Jolene wanted to pull her hand away, but she liked the way it felt too much, the warm tingle it sent up her arm and the way it made her pulse skitter. "I'm okay. That was freaky, though."

"I would have come myself, but Sarah is better at that sort of thing. I'm not good with vortexes." Mateo squeezed her hand. "So now do you believe in witches?"

"Witches? No. I'm not even sure Sarah *is* a witch. All she did was pull us out of the vortex. No spells. No charms. No bats' wings or toads. She must have some sort of a paranormal energy gift that makes her immune to the vortex and allows her to pull people out." Jolene wondered why he kept harping on witches, and why she was so determined not to believe in them. Was *he* a witch?

Mateo's smile was patient. "I guess you still need time." He stepped closer, his thumb tracing her cheek, lifting her chin up so that she was looking into those deep, soulful eyes of his. "I was thinking maybe we could—"

"So this is where we ... Oh." Celeste had run up to them but her eyes grew wide, darting between the two of them. "Sorry. Did I interrupt something?"

"Yes," Mateo said.

"No." Jolene scowled at him.

"I can come back later." Celeste started to turn around, but Fiona and Morgan came up beside her with their faces buried in their cellphones.

"We were looking at the map and correlating the old Salem Village to the GPS here on Google. Clearly, we're not in the right place or maybe Sam's house is in the vortex."

"What makes you think it's out here in the first place?" Mateo asked, turning his attention away from Jolene.

"We found that his house was on West Great River Road, but when we went there in Salem, it was a pharmacy," Celeste said.

"But then we discovered that we were looking in the wrong place. We were looking in modern day Salem and we should have been in old Salem Village," Jolene explained.

"But the street we had for him didn't exist on the map we had." Morgan pointed to the 1692 map replica in her hand.

"So, we went to the Ephemera Museum where they had more detailed maps and we found the street," Fiona told Mateo.

"That river over there used to be called the Great River." Jolene pointed to the path they'd come back on. "That used to be a road that ran along the river. We figure it was West Great River Road, since it's west of the river. According to our research, that is the road that Sam Gooding's house was on."

Mateo pursed his lips in thought. "I see, but there's not really a road here. Just this narrow deer path. And there are no houses."

"I guess there was a road and houses three hundred years ago," Celeste said. "It's all overgrown now."

"Or you're looking in the wrong place. I don't think his house would have been near the vortex. This vortex is ancient. It's been here forever." Mateo pointed at the woods. "That's why this piece of land has never been developed. People come here and they get a funny feeling, and then they aren't so keen to go through with development plans. Even when they make plans, the plans always fall through."

"Well, if his house wasn't here, then where was it?" Jolene asked.

Mateo frowned at the map. "It looks like there is a road here on the other side of the river."

"But that's the east side of the river," Fiona pointed out.

"Right. Here it is." Mateo traced the windy river with his finger. "But here the river winds like a snake. It's actually southwest from where we are right now, but the section of land inside this hairpin turn is dead west. I say we go look there."

Morgan shrugged and looked at the GPS map on her phone. "It does look like there is a road that used to cut through there. It's worth a try."

"Yes, and we have plenty of time to do it. Sarah got rid of the paranormals that were following you buying you some time," Mateo said.

"Do you think the bearded guys she mentioned were the people who have been following us all along?" Jolene asked Morgan.

Morgan glanced around. "Possibly. I don't feel anyone following us now. I want to think it was always Sarah."

"There's a bridge at the fork in the road. We could drive across the bridge then park in the woods and walk along the river." Mateo glanced up at the clear blue sky. "It's a nice day."

"What the heck," Fiona said. "I agree with Mateo. Besides, we're already here and we don't have any other leads."

"Sure." Jolene shrugged. "What have we got to lose?"

Chapter 19

Mateo was right. On the other side of the river there was a much wider path. It was overgrown, but it was more like the width of a three-hundred-year-old road than the path they were following before.

Jolene enjoyed the quiet peacefulness of the woods. Squirrels rustled in the leaves and birds flew between pine branches. The river bubbled alongside the road. It was a warm day, above eighty degrees, but the tall oak, maple and pine trees provided a canopy of shade which made the journey pleasantly comfortable.

What made it even more pleasant was the way Mateo had easily grabbed her hand and laced his fingers through hers as if it were the most natural thing in the world.

Jolene struggled to keep the flush from her face when she spotted her sisters' knowing glances. They all had guys in their lives—why shouldn't she? Except she really didn't *have* Mateo in her life, did she? She glanced up at him, his handsome profile dark and mysterious. Would he stick around long enough to actually *be* in her life? Did she even want that?

They rounded a corner and, as if by magic, the woods cleared enough to reveal an old, sagging house. It was simple in style, two stories and clad in wooden boards, some of which were now hanging off. The windows were small, most of them boarded up. A brick chimney that stuck up from the middle of the house was crumbling. Bricks lay on the roof and scattered around the house along with slate shingles that had come loose from the roof. The yard had been reclaimed by the forest, giving the house the appearance of having sprung up in the middle of the woods.

"This must be Sam's house!" Jolene took off at a trot toward the house. Excitement bubbled up inside her. She was only twenty feet away from the house that might possibly have the scrying ball hidden inside.

Twang!

A bolt of electricity zinged through her body. The next thing she knew she was flat on her back on the ground.

"Whoa. Watch out there, Jolene," Morgan, who had jogged up behind her, teased. "Did you trip on something?"

But she hadn't tripped. It was more like she'd walked into an electrified brick wall. A force field. She held her hands out to stop Morgan. "Hold up. There's something weird going on here."

Morgan frowned but kept walking. "What? I don't—"

Twang!

Morgan jumped back. "Whoa! What the heck was *that*?" She reached her hand out tentatively to touch what looked like thin air.

Twang!

Morgan jerked her hand back and shook it. "That hurt."

The others had stopped beside them, eyeing the space between them and the house. Mateo helped Jolene up. She dusted dried leaves and pine needles off her jeans as she stared at the house. Now that she was looking, she could see a slight shimmer in the air.

Fiona picked up a rock and tossed it. It sizzled for a split second as it passed through the invisible barrier and landed on the other side.

"It looks like some kind of an energy barrier."

"I wonder if it goes all around the house." Celeste walked to the left, along the edge of the invisible wall. When she got fifty feet along, she reached out a tentative finger.

"*Twang!*"

"Looks like it does," Morgan said.

"Well, that's good news and bad news," Celeste said. "The good news is that this is probably the place we're looking for and it is well protected. The bad news is that we can't get in."

"And even more bad news." Fiona pointed at a patch of ground near the invisible wall where the leaves had been pushed away. Their eyes followed it—all along the wall the leaves and growth had been disturbed. "Someone else has been here."

"Someone looking for the crystal ball." Morgan walked the length of the wall. "But it looks like they didn't get in."

Jolene could see the scuff marks were only on their side, but someone had tried the same thing they were trying. That person had also walked along the perimeter to try to find a way in. Had they found it? She raised her energy awareness to look at the energy trail. "It's the same energy signature that I saw at Amity Jones' house."

"So, the person—or persons—that killed Nancy was here." Morgan looked around nervously.

"And they were possibly the killers of Opal," Fiona added.

"Hopefully, they were the bearded paranormals that Sarah did away with," Celeste suggested. "It's a safe bet they were sent by Bly and we know he is after the scrying ball."

"If it was them, he'll send someone else soon enough. But we do owe Sarah a lot since she got them out of the way," Jolene said.

"And don't forget how she saved us from the vortex," Morgan reminded them.

"True. We should get her a nice gift," Jolene said.

"*Meow!*"

The black cat, Raven, appeared on the other side of the invisible wall. She trotted over to the house and rubbed her cheek against a corner, then looked back at them smugly.

"Hey, how did the cat get in there?" Fiona asked.

"There must be a way in! A hole in the force field or something. We need to go all around the perimeter and see if we can find it. I'll go this way. Celeste, you go the other way." Jolene started to the right.

Merow!

Jolene and her sisters were surprised to see Belladonna come running out from behind the house. Their cat trotted straight toward them, her ice blue eyes sparkling. She was getting uncomfortably close to the invisible wall and not slowing down.

"Stop!" Jolene put her hand out, as if Belladonna would obey her command. But the cat never took instructions from humans and this was no exception.

Belladonna did not slow down.

Jolene's chest constricted as Belladonna reached the force field. "No, Belladonna, go back!" She held her breath in anticipation of the cat hitting the electric charge. She hoped it wouldn't hurt her too badly.

Instead of being hurt, Belladonna simply walked right through it as if nothing were there. She rubbed her head on Jolene's ankle.

"Hey, she went right through it." Jolene bent down to pet her. "Maybe there's a hole that we can get through right here." She reached out to touch the area Belladonna had just passed through.

Twang!

"I guess not."

"*Merowph*!" Belladonna twitched her tail and trotted off back toward the house, passing through the invisible force field as if it had no effect on her. She looked back at the sisters as if wondering why they didn't follow her.

Fiona waved her hand at the invisible wall. "I guess cats are immune to whatever it is."

"There has to be a way to get through. This has got to be some sort of paranormal energy field." Morgan turned to Jolene. "You're the strongest. Why not try to tap into your energy gifts to see if you can break it or unlock it somehow?"

Jolene scrunched up her face and, raising her awareness as high as she could, she focused on the wall. But nothing happened.

Mateo had been standing back with his arms crossed watching the girls in silence. "Why don't you just use the spell?"

"The spell? What good would that do?" Jolene asked.

"I think the force field is a charm. Someone put it on this house a long time ago so no one could get in," Mateo said. "Clearly they made it only effective for humans."

Morgan's eyes flicked from Mateo to the invisible wall. "But it's energy. We can counteract it somehow with our paranormal powers."

"First, let's make sure we are actually in the right place." Fiona dug into her pocket. "Counteracting that could be a real drain on our energy. We don't want to do that unless we really need to get in there. If there are other paranormals around, we might need all our skills to fight them. It would be just like Bly to let us use up our energy to break the force field and then take us in our weakened state."

Jolene could see before Fiona's fist even cleared her pocket that they were in the right place. The alexandrite keystone was glowing so brightly that beams of orange light spread out from the spaces between Fiona's fingers.

And then the solution hit her.

Jolene grabbed the alexandrite from Fiona. "We don't need a spell." Holding the stone between her forefinger and thumb she stepped up to the wall and thrust it out into the energy field like a key being thrust into a lock.

Click.

The air shimmered.

The hair on Jolene's arms tickled with static electricity.

She handed the stone back to Fiona, and then stepped over the threshold of the invisible barrier and headed for the house.

Chapter 20

Silenced weighed heavy in the air as the sisters and Mateo approached the house. It was as if the space near the house absorbed the normal woodland sounds, like they were hearing everything from inside a pillow.

The house drew them toward it. The cockeyed pieces of wooden siding that hung from the front seemed to beckon them. The windows, or at least the ones that weren't boarded up, stared at them like dark, expectant eyes. Most of the brown paint had flaked off the house long ago, but the large oak door with its giant cast-iron latch remained almost as good as the day it was made.

Jolene got a sense that the house had been waiting for them for almost three hundred years. Not unwelcoming, but not welcoming either. Just waiting. Jolene was glad Mateo caught up with her and linked his fingers with hers. It gave her strength and made her feel powerful.

Morgan was the first to plant her foot firmly on the old granite porch. She curled her hand around the latch. "I don't suppose we'd be lucky enough to find the door unlocked." She clicked the latch and pushed.

The door creaked open.

Jolene stood on her tiptoes to get a look inside over Morgan's shoulder. Two of the windows on the side were not boarded up and they sent shafts of golden light into the dim room. Centuries-old dust floated in the air, illuminated by the slices of light.

It had been a nice home. The inside still had the original moldings and fixtures which were much better preserved than the exterior of the house. Inside nothing stirred. The only movement was a flurry of dust that swirled in the air from when Morgan had opened the door.

"I think it's safe to go in." Morgan stepped inside.

They all followed her in and the wooden floor groaned, protesting the weight of people standing on it after three hundred years. Jolene could see the room they were in took up most of the front of the house. It was devoid of furniture. Had Sam moved out at one point? What had happened to Sam anyway? Jolene had never found the answer to any of that in her research.

An opening on the far left led to what looked like the remains of a kitchen, though she could only see a few shelves. To the right of that was a stairway. Some of the stair boards were missing, but the wide baluster leading to a fancy newel post at the bottom was still intact. The newel post was unusually intricate for a colonial home and was adorned with mythical faces carved in high relief, culminating in a round orb at the top. But it wasn't so much the stairs that caught her eye, it was the brick fireplace. It was the same exact fireplace she'd seen in Sam Gooding's sketch.

"That's the same fireplace that's in Sam's sketch. The scrying ball must be hidden in the fireplace somewhere!"

The sisters rushed to the fireplace, the pads of their fingers pressing on the rough bricks, looking for a loose stone or hidden compartment. Their fingernails chipped at the crumbling mortar. Their activity released the smells of ash and cold air.

"Where would it be? I don't see any hidden compartment." Morgan bent down to inspect the large hearth stone. "Do you suppose it's up the chimney?"

Jolene stepped back and looked at the blackened hearth. It was almost large enough to stand in and still had a black cast-iron pot hanging on a hook. The chimney would be a good hiding place. Sam could have made a compartment inside. But she didn't relish the idea of going up there to find out.

"Why don't you point the crystal at it, Fiona, and we'll see if it gives us any indication as to where the scrying ball might be."

Fiona stepped back a few paces and pointed the crystal at the hearth.

It barely changed color.

She waved it over the face of the fireplace, the glow turning from gray to yellow to blue to red. "It's glowing more towards that end of the fireplace." Fiona aimed it toward the section of the fireplace that was next to the stairs.

"Wait a minute," Mateo said. "Maybe it's not in the fireplace at all. It glows hotter when it's pointed near the stairs."

Fiona shifted position, gliding the stone past the fireplace and over to the stairs. It sparked bright orange.

"It must be upstairs," Celeste said.

"But the sketch was of this room," Jolene pointed out.

Morgan pressed her lips together. "Maybe he made more than one sketch, to show a progression of where to go in the house. And maybe we only got the first sketch that leads us toward the stairs. We never saw the whole diary."

Jolene thought about the sketch. "You could be right. I thought it was the fireplace because that seems like a place where one might hide something, but the sketch does show the stairs as prominently as the fireplace."

"We might as well look upstairs. We can always come back to this." Celeste gestured toward the fireplace.

"Anything is better than climbing into the chimney." Jolene started toward the stairs.

They clambered up the stairs, careful to avoid the missing and rotted boards. The upstairs hallway had three doors, all leading to rooms with rough pine flooring and paint-chipped walls.

"*Mew!*" Belladonna appeared in the doorway of one of the rooms.

"Might as well start in there." Morgan was the first to cross into the small room. It was empty aside from a tattered remnant of a dirty curtain that fluttered listlessly in an open window. The walls, which had once been white, were now tinged green with mold. Below the window, a deep brown water stain covered what was left of the horsehair plaster. Moss clung to the windowsill where a small sapling had taken root. The cracked and water-stained ceilings bulged alarmingly in the corner.

The floorboards creaked as the five of them stood looking around the room.

"*Meurffp.*" Raven paced back and forth in the corner that abutted the stairs.

"Where would someone hide a crystal ball in here?" Fiona spun slowly around. "There's no place to hide anything. It's just an empty room."

"*Breeee!*" Belladonna and Raven trotted to the corner of the room and rubbed their cheeks on the doorjamb.

"Looks like Belladonna found a friend," Celeste said. "That looks like Sarah's cat. I wonder if she's around here and if she's helping Belladonna escape for whatever reason."

"If Sarah is near here, I hope she has an idea of where Sam might have hidden the crystal ball." Jolene walked over to a section of wall where the plaster had fallen off, exposing the studs underneath. She peered down inside the wall. "Because the only idea I have is to tear off the plaster and look inside the walls."

"And under the floorboards." Morgan pried up a loose board in the corner.

Fiona aimed the alexandrite around the room. It sparked when she pointed it toward the front corner of the room, where Belladonna and Raven where sitting, leisurely cleaning themselves.

"Well, at least that narrows it down. Let's focus over here." Fiona shoved the stone back in her pocket as they all went toward the corner.

"*Merow!*"

"*Hiss!*"

The two cats swatted at each other, rolling on the ground and then leaping to the side. Then they ran out of the room and down the stairs.

Jolene stared after them. "I guess they've done their job. I suppose we should get to work."

"Right." Celeste squatted and tapped on a floorboard. "Let's see if we can find an obvious hollow area before we start ripping the place up."

The sisters got to work, tapping on the walls and searching the floors for variation in the wood planks that might indicate some sort of trap door or hidden compartment.

Mateo stayed by Jolene's side, helping her pry up the dry floorboards. Then he showed her what to listen for when tapping the wall, where to hold her ear and the type of thud she should be listening for. They didn't find a secret compartment, but Jolene realized she liked having him by her side... more than she wanted to admit.

Over an hour later, they'd demolished a good part of the room with nothing to show for it. The temperature had climbed to unbearable levels and Jolene pushed damp tendrils of hair out of her eyes as she sat back on her haunches to rest. She was shamelessly admiring the way Mateo's damp t-shirt clung to his muscular chest when she noticed that Morgan was acting a bit edgy.

"What's wrong?" Fiona wiped sweat from her brow.

"I sense something … like we might not be alone," Morgan said.

Jolene stood. "I thought Sarah took care of Bly's men."

Moran shrugged. "Maybe they weren't the only ones looking for the crystal ball."

Jolene crossed to the window and scanned the woods. "I feel something, too. I don't see anyone, and this place has a weird energy vibe. Probably something to do with that energy shield Sam Gooding put around it. Maybe we're just imagining it."

"Maybe," Morgan said. "I'm not imagining that there's no scrying ball here."

"I know. Now I wonder if coming up here was a mistake," Jolene said.

"But the crystal lit up when I pointed upstairs and it is now lighting up when I point it at this corner." Fiona pointed to the corner which was now bare studs.

"Sure, that's the direction the crystal is pointed in, but does that mean it's in *this* room?" Celeste asked.

"*Merow*!" A dual cat cry echoed from the stairwell just outside the room.

"No, it could be pointing at what's *beyond* the room on the other side of the wall," Mateo said.

"The stairs! We should have thought of that before." Jolene slapped her hand against her thigh. "The stairs are in Sam's sketch. They were the clue all along, not the fireplace."

They scrambled out into the stairwell. Belladonna and Raven sat at the bottom, staring up at them expectantly.

"The cats were trying to lead us here the whole time." Jolene joined the cats perched on the second step. The one below it was missing the tread and she looked down into the dark hole below the stairs.

Celeste looked over her shoulder. "Maybe it's down in there, below the planks."

Jolene felt a shiver of energy. "In the basement? Does this place even have a basement?"

"They didn't have basements as we know it three hundred years ago, but there might be a root cellar or a low cellar hole. Probably a dirt floor. Maybe he buried it down there. I'm not sure if there's access to it from in here, though," Morgan said. "Maybe there's a bulkhead outside."

"But look at the stairs." Fiona gestured toward the broken boards. "Maybe someone else already came here and figured it out. They crawled into the basement through the stairs and dug up the scrying ball."

"We did see that someone had been at the invisible wall," Celeste said.

"Yeah, but they didn't get in," Morgan pointed out.

"That doesn't mean that someone else didn't get in here. If this was Sam's house, then it's been here for three-hundred years," Jolene said. "That's a long time for the crystal ball to be sitting here. There would have been plenty of opportunities for someone to try to snag it."

"Then why is the gemstone glowing?" Fiona asked.

"And why do I feel like a threat is here?" Morgan said uneasily.

"Are you sure there's a threat?" Jolene asked.

Morgan paused and closed her eyes. "No, I'm not sure. Maybe you're right and it's just the funky energy here."

Jolene went back to the top of the stairs and looked out the window at the end of the hall. The sun was low in the sky now. It would be setting soon and then it would be dark. The house had no electricity and the thought of being out there in the middle of the woods in the dark didn't appeal to her.

"I don't see anyone out there—" Was that the flapping edge of something black disappearing behind a tree? "Unless that's a familiar black tunic flapping like a cape out there."

"Sarah?" Mateo asked. "She might be here watching over us. Protecting you."

"I guess that would make sense." Morgan didn't look convinced.

Celeste pointed at the fluffy black cat. "Her cat is here, so it does make sense. Hopefully, that's the presence you're feeling."

"It's going to be getting dark soon. I think we should either pick up the pace or come back tomorrow." Jolene pulled her hair up off her neck and exhaled heavily.

"*Meow.*" Belladonna trotted up the steps and head-butted Jolene's leg. She turned and trotted down the bottom of the stairs where the black cat was staring up at them with unwavering, golden eyes.

"*Merophh!*"

"I think she's trying to tell us something, as usual." Morgan descended the stairs and stood in the middle of the room. "This is where Sam made the sketch, but I don't remember the exact perspectives."

Jolene and the others came down to stand beside Morgan. "I do." She anchored herself in the middle of the room where she could see the edge of the fireplace and the stairway. "This is the exact perspective. That's why I thought it was in the fireplace."

"Okay, so then we've been on the wrong—" Morgan's eyes drifted out the window, her expression turning ominous.

"Is everything okay?" The hair on the back of Jolene's neck prickled and she looked out the window, too.

Morgan's attention snapped back to the room. "Yeah. Fine. I just thought ... never mind. Anyway, you were saying this is the perspective. But somehow we're off. We've tried the fireplace and the room upstairs. It must be in the chimney."

Fiona got out the alexandrite stone and aimed it around the room, walking slowly, using it like a Geiger counter to ferret out the crystal ball. She walked past the fireplace and the stone turned yellow. At the edge of the stairs, the stone glowed a yellow-orange. Just past the stairs, the crystal exploded into a fiery ball of orangey-red. "It's got to be somewhere around here. Look at the crystal!"

"*Merow*!" Belladonna jumped up onto the baluster, sliding down comically and landing in a heap at the bottom of the newel post.

Scratch.

"What's that?" Celeste turned toward the front door.

"I don't know, but look at the stone now." Fiona's attention was focused on the alexandrite whose beams of light glowed brighter as she pointed it toward the stairs.

Everyone turned from the front door to the stone.

"But we already looked at the stairs," Jolene said.

"Not the stairs." Fiona walked slowly toward them. "It's the—"

"*Merow!*" Belladonna leaped up onto the newel post.

"*Hiss!*" Raven leaped up there, too. The two cats hissed and meowed as they grappled for position on the post. Their razor sharp claws scrambled for purchase on the rounded top, but they kept slipping off.

Jolene stared in amazement as the resulting scratches on the globe at the top of the newel post emitted shards of silvery light as if something inside was glowing.

The cats catapulted off the top, running around the room in a noisy, mewling frenzy.

Jolene's attention was riveted on the top of the post. She walked slowly over to it. "Do you think this is..." She touched the ball atop the post.

Electricity lit up her nerves all the way from her finger to her elbow. Flakes of paint flew off the top of the globe, revealing what was inside: a crystal ball.

Jolene placed both her hands on the ball and pulled it from the post. Holding it in front of her face, she peered inside it. It was like watching a movie, a movie of the outside of the very house they were now in. A man was skulking around the perimeter, dragging something heavy behind him, making his way to the front door.

"Hey, this looks like the guy from the Ephemera Museum and he's right outside the—"

Crash!

The door flew open, smashing against the wall.

"Hand over the crystal ball or the witch gets it!"

Chapter 21

Jolene's heart somersaulted in her chest. Henry Oaks stood in the doorway. He no longer looked like a meek museum curator, especially considering the way he was dragging an unconscious Sarah behind him.

The sight of Sarah—unconscious ... or worse —was disturbing enough, but what really struck an icicle of fear into Jolene's heart was the unusual looking gun he held in one hand.

It wasn't a regular gun, though Jolene could see he had one of those tucked in his waistband. This was a gun that could shoot paranormal energy. Jolene and her sisters had had to fight off men with guns like that before. If the gun was filled with dark energy, it could be deadly.

Jolene's heart sank as she remembered the dark energy she'd felt at the museum when looking through the photocopies on Sam Gooding. The energy hadn't been from Sam, it had been from Henry. Henry had handled those papers before giving them to Jolene.

If only she'd been a little more on the ball instead of mooning over Mateo, she might have figured out what he was up to in time to avoid this mess.

Fighting this guy was going to take all of her concentration. Jolene slid her eyes to Celeste, holding the ball out so her sister would take it while she turned up her energy awareness.

Henry's eyes followed the ball like a turkey vulture tracking a wounded baby rabbit. "Oh, no. You give that to me." He jerked the gun in Jolene's direction just as she handed the scrying ball off to Celeste.

"So, *you* were the one following us!" Morgan said, distracting Henry from the ball.

A sly smile spread across Henry's face. "You detected me? I didn't think you guys would notice, especially when you seemed so oblivious when I ran into you on the street near your hotel."

"You were onto us all along," Fiona said.

"Not *all* along. I've been looking for the scrying ball for my entire career." Henry's eyes slid to the ball, then back to Morgan. "But I never knew who'd hidden it back in 1692. When you came in asking about Sam Gooding, I didn't think anything about it at first. But then I did some research and I realized you were on to something."

"And you sent us to the vortex on purpose to get rid of us so you could come here to Sam's house," Morgan said.

Henry laughed. "Yes. When you came with the map, I realized the same thing you did. Sam's house wasn't in modern day Salem. And I knew exactly where West Great River Road was. But I couldn't let you come *here* ... so I made up that story about the road being to the west and sent you to the vortex. It was supposed to swallow you up and leave me free to come here and get the crystal ball."

"But Sarah saved us, and you couldn't get near the house." Jolene wanted to keep him talking while she focused on her gifts. She needed to figure out a way to zap him with an energy stream that would knock him out without harming Sarah.

"That's right! The darn house was protected by an energy field charm. And my warlock abilities aren't quite up to snuff ... so I couldn't get in. But then it all worked out for the best because you came and unlocked the energy charm."

Henry's eyes shifted to the alexandrite in Fiona's hand. "I would have needed that to unlock it and to find the scrying ball. I knew the keystone existed. Too bad I couldn't find it in your hotel room."

"It was you who broke in?" Morgan said. "I suppose you also killed Nancy and Opal."

"And maybe even Amity," Jolene added.

Henry gestured with the gun, his eyes narrowing. "I didn't kill anybody. Not yet, anyway."

Everyone's eyes flicked to Sarah's limp body that he was still holding by the back of her tunic.

Henry looked down. "She's not dead. But she's gonna be if you don't hand over that crystal ball."

Jolene couldn't believe that the whole time she'd been thinking some bad guy paranormal was following them it had been this little old guy from the museum.

But that couldn't be right, because he didn't catch on to them until they went into the Ephemera Museum, which meant someone else must have been following them, too.

Jolene looked down at his energy trail. It wasn't the same as the one she'd seen at Amity Jones' house. Maybe the paranormals who killed Nancy and Opal really were the ones Sarah had gotten rid of.

Henry narrowed his eyes at Celeste. "Are you going to hand over the crystal ball, Blondie, or shall I fry the witch?" He pressed the paranormal gun to Sarah's head.

Jolene saw Mateo flinch next to her. They couldn't let Henry hurt Sarah. She'd saved them from the vortex. They owed her everything.

Celeste cried out, "Wait!" She held the crystal ball out toward Henry. "Don't hurt her."

Henry let go of Sarah and she slumped to the floor. He turned the paranormal gun on Celeste "That's right. You come right over here and give it to me."

Celeste inched forward toward Henry.

Jolene glanced at Mateo. She really wanted to send a jolt of energy in Henry's direction, but he had that gun pointed at Celeste and she was afraid he'd shoot before she could take him out. But she and Mateo had proven before that they had strong energy together. Maybe if they combined their energy, they could hit Henry before he had a chance to react.

It was as if Mateo knew what she was thinking. He reached out and took Jolene's hand.

The movement caught Henry's eye. He whipped the real gun out from his waistband and pointed it at them.

"What are you doing over there?" Henry's eyes wavered from Celeste to Jolene and Mateo. "No monkey business or I'll send an energy jolt through the blonde that will cook her from the inside out like a TV dinner in a microwave."

Mateo held up the palm of his free hand. "Sorry."

With his other hand, he squeezed Jolene's in a silent signal. She took a deep breath focusing all her energy—and some of Mateo's—on her fingertips, which she flung out toward Henry.

Everything happened in slow motion.

Henry jerked the paranormal gun over to meet the stream of purple energy coming from Jolene.

"*Meow*!" Belladonna and Raven launched themselves at Henry.

Henry's eyes jerked from the energy stream to the cats. Still aiming the paranormal gun at the energy stream he pulled the trigger. A glob of red energy lurched out, meeting the purple energy and exploding into a white arc.

He aimed the real gun at the cats.

Bang! Bang! Bang!

In her heightened paranormal state, with everything slowed down, Jolene could see the trajectory of the bullets. One of them was heading straight for Belladonna's heart.

"No!" Jolene dived for Belladonna, pushing her out of the way of the bullet, but unfortunately forgetting that, as she was pushing the cat out of the bullet's path, she was putting herself straight in it.

"Look out!" Jolene heard Mateo yell the words at the same time she saw his body lurch in between her and the bullets.

They struck him dead center in the chest and he collapsed to the floor.

***

Jolene's heart crashed as she stared down at Mateo. Unaware of anything that was going on around her, her attention was riveted on Mateo, who lay on his back on the ground. Blood bubbled out of the three holes in his chest. So much blood.

She forgot all about Henry and the scrying ball as panic jolted her out of her trance. She had to do something to save him. Fiona's healing carnelians. She'd experienced their healing power herself, although not with such a life-threatening wound.

Fiona was looking at Mateo with wide eyes while fumbling in her pocket. It took forever for her to pull the orange stones out. She bent down and placed them on Mateo's chest. She looked up at Jolene and shook her head.

Jolene could already see that Mateo's face was turning white. The spreading pool of blood underneath him was leaching all the color—and life—out of him. She could see his energy draining out as well. It spread over the floor in a bright, aqua puddle.

The stones weren't working. The wounds were too severe. She knew from when they'd found Nancy, already dead, that the stones wouldn't pull someone back. But Mateo wasn't dead ... at least not yet. Jolene refused to give up hope. Her gifts were powerful. She could do the healing work even if the stones couldn't.

Jolene knew they were in danger of losing the scrying ball, and probably a lot more, to Henry but she didn't care about that. There was nothing else in the room for her but Mateo. She pushed Fiona aside and threw herself on top of him.

Jolene focused all her energy on the life-depleting wounds. She could feel Mateo's vibration weakening. The energy drain was slowing, but he was still losing it quicker than she could stop it from coming out. The only solution was more energy going in. Her energy.

She pushed her energy into him, focusing on his veins, pushing her own life force though them, straight to his heart. It stuttered once. Twice. And then no more.

Her own heart shattered. She was losing him! Her gifts, powerful as they were, were not enough. She needed something more powerful. Something with unlimited power.

Through the haze of her grief, she heard Sarah's voice. "Chant the spell."

The spell! Cassiopeia had said the spell had unlimited power and that it could help boost their own powers, but she wasn't sure how to use it. She knew she would have to say it with all her heart, but was there a certain way to do that?

Why hadn't she paid more attention?

Mateo had said something about being able to help them boost the spell, but now he was unconscious. She would have to make it work on her own.

She dug deep within herself. Deep down to the bottom of her heart. She focused on heartfelt intent and said the words:

By Water, Earth, Air and Fire,
I ask thee now grant my desire,
Harming none I now decree
This charm is done, so mote it be

She repeated the spell over and over while focusing on pushing her energy into Mateo. She felt herself weakening as her own energy seeped out of her and into Mateo. She focused on filling his veins, pushing the energy to his heart so that it would start beating again. Filling him with life even as it drained out of her.

The last thing Jolene was aware of before her own energy faded out was Mateo's heart thudding back to life with one faint beat.

***

Celeste cradled the crystal ball to her chest. With all the crazy energy floating around, she didn't know what was going to happen and she wanted to protect it. Especially from the white-hot sparks that had resulted from the explosion when the purple and red energy arcs met.

To her left, Jolene had thrown herself on top of Mateo. Celeste could see that Mateo needed her sister's undivided attention. But Jolene was the most powerful paranormal of the sisters, and she was now out of commission. The girls would have to fight Henry themselves, Celeste thought ruefully as she watched Henry aim his paranormal gun at her.

Sarah lay unmoving at Henry's feet. Morgan rushed to her side, pulling her away from the commotion and checking her for wounds.

Fiona pulled her fisted hand out of her pocket, the glow of the rocks inside escaping from between her fingers. She raised her fist and flung the rocks at Henry.

Henry's eyes went wide as he saw the red, glowing projectiles flying toward him like comets. He was a lot spryer than he let on when shuffling around town and the museum, so he actually managed to shoot the stone down with the paranormal gun.

Fiona whipped her head around in a panic. Celeste figured she was looking around for more stones that she could throw but there were none.

"Now you're pissing me off." Henry changed a setting on the gun and aimed it at Fiona.

"No!" Celeste screamed as greenish-yellow strands of energy flew out of the gun.

The strands wrapped themselves around Fiona like snakes. Fiona writhed and struggled but she was constrained by the energy. Henry aimed the gun at Morgan and Sarah on the floor near him and fired, with the same results.

"These energy strands will grow tighter and tighter like a python strangling the life out of them." He stepped closer to Celeste and held out his free hand. "Put the crystal ball in my hand and I'll leave you to free your sisters. Otherwise, you'll meet the same fate and you'll all die here."

Celeste clutched the ball closer. Of all the sisters, she was the one with no defensive powers. She struggled to see Henry's spirit. Sometimes she could see people's spirits and those spirits would help her defend herself, but with Henry she saw nothing.

Jolene didn't appear to be aware of what was going on around them. The way she was laying there so still and pale made Celeste's heart break. Without the help of her sisters' paranormal gifts, Celeste had no chance against Henry. Not unless she suddenly came up with something more powerful ... something with unlimited power.

Celeste felt something wrap around her ankle. She looked down. Sarah's hand! Celeste glanced at Sarah's face and their eyes locked. "Chant the spell-I'll help you boost the power."

The spell!

Cassiopeia had said the spell had unlimited power. But she'd have to say it with heartfelt intent. Her eyes flicked to Mateo, deathly pale and unconscious. He'd said he could help boost it, but was in no condition to do that now. Celeste was the least powerful, but maybe with Sarah's help the boost would be enough.

She looked down at the crystal ball, then to her sisters and Sarah who were struggling against the ropes of energy. She was their only hope. She dug deep down and focused with all her heart.

By Water, Earth, Air and Fire,
I ask thee now grant my desire,
Harming none I now decree
This charm is done, so mote it be

As soon as the words left her lips, Celeste felt a rush of power. A deafening whooshing sound filled the house. It sounded as if a jet plane engine was revving up inside the chimney. A harsh wind whipped down the stairs, straight to the hearth where leaves swirled and black ash puffed out into the room.

And then she saw the ghosts. A dozen of them swirling and whipping around. They screeched at full speed toward Henry, encircling him in a swirl of angry mist.

Henry screamed, his face contorting in fear. Apparently, Henry could see ghosts, too. But who were they? Celeste thought they looked like witches. The witches of the Salem ghosts, maybe? Apparently, Henry had done something they didn't like. Had the spell brought them here?

The ghosts pulled at him with gnarled, bony fingers. Henry's eyes darted back and forth. He struggled to free himself from the witches' grasp, but to no avail.

Henry let out an earth-shattering scream. The paranormal gun he still held in his hand exploded into a million white-hot pieces and at the same time the energy binds that held Fiona, Morgan and Sarah shimmered and disappeared.

Through it all, Celeste clutched the crystal ball.

***

Henry lay curled into a ball on the floor, rocking and babbling as the spirits swirled around him.

"Who are they?" Celeste asked Sarah, who was now wide awake and sitting up.

"Ghosts of witches. Henry was a witch, but he broke his vow. He turned to the dark side. The witches have been waiting for three hundred years to insure the scrying ball gets into the hands where it belongs." Sarah pointed to the sisters. "The crystal ball is where it should be now. Under your protection."

"We need to call an ambulance for Mateo and Jolene." Morgan knelt beside them. She pressed two fingers on Jolene's wrist and then did the same to Mateo. "They both have pulses, but very faint."

Fiona already had her phone out and had called 911. She gave the dispatcher the GPS of their location in the woods, as her phone reported it, and told her they needed an ambulance as quickly as possible. When she heard sirens split the air, she ended the call. She glanced out the front door and saw a police car speed through the overgrown path, mowing down shrubs and tall grass. Fiona watched in amazement as Detective Peterson got out of the car and ran to the front door. He stood there just staring in confusion at the mess.

Celeste wasn't surprised at the confused look on his face. On one side of the room, Jolene and Mateo lay in a heap on the floor. On the other side, Henry was curled in a ball, babbling incoherently. Sarah sat stroking Raven who purred in her lap. Belladonna flitted nervously between Morgan and Fiona, who both looked a bit disheveled from the energy ropes.

"What is going on here?" Peterson demanded to know.

Celeste held the crystal ball, nonchalantly hiding the glowing piece where the paint had flaked off against her side and hoping Peterson would be too distracted with everything else going on to ask questions about it.

Sarah pointed to Henry. "He's crazy. He came busting in here and shot that man."

Peterson's eyes widened as he noticed the dark stain under Mateo. "He's bleeding bad. What about the woman?" Without waiting for an answer, he pressed the microphone on his lapel. "I need an ambulance at the old West Great River Road. Right away."

Peterson turned to the girls. "Just what were you people doing here? This house is in the middle of nowhere. Why would you come here ... and did you break in?"

"We thought it was part of the Salem witch trial history. We found out about it on the Internet," Celeste blurted out, her eyes fixed on Jolene who Morgan was tending to.

She didn't have time for Peterson's questions. Her sister was in trouble!

"And you broke in?" Peterson's tone was incredulous. "I'm sure you could see the house is abandoned and not exactly open for visitors, or safe."

"Look, can you wait with the questions? My sister is—"

Morgan was interrupted by sirens and flashing red lights. The ambulance! Peterson looked out the door in surprise at their impossibly quick arrival.

They all watched helplessly as the paramedics worked on Jolene and Mateo.

"Will they be okay?" Morgan asked.

"Not sure. They're weak but stable. We need to get them to the hospital pronto," one of the ambulance attendants told Morgan as they loaded Jolene and Mateo onto stretchers.

Morgan followed behind the stretcher. "I'll go with—"

"No, you won't!" Peterson shot out his arm to stop her.

"What? But I—"

"Things look very suspicious here." Peterson's eyes scanned the room. "I'll need your statement first. Then you can go."

Morgan's eyes flicked to the ambulance, but they were already closing the back door.

Fiona touched her arm. "She's in good hands. She'll be fine."

Morgan sighed and turned back. "Fine. Ask away."

The next twenty minutes were filled with Peterson asking a bunch of questions while two policemen hauled away Henry and crime lab techs took pictures.

Celeste tried to rein in her impatience. The urge to rush to Jolene's side as well as get the scrying ball safely out of there was strong. She spent most of the time avoiding looking at the bloodstain on the floor and hoping that Mateo had not lost too much blood to survive.

At a certain point, Peterson relayed word from the hospital that Mateo and Jolene would be fine, which made Celeste feel a little better. Even more so when it appeared that he seemed not to have noticed the scrying ball at all.

Finally, the police packed up their stuff and left. Peterson was the last out the door, giving them a stern warning to get out of the woods before dark.

"I want to thank you guys for saving me," Sarah said to Fiona, Morgan and Celeste.

"One good turn deserves another. You pulled us out of the vortex," Morgan replied. "But what were you doing here?"

"I was watching over you. Hanging back outside. Henry is a member of the witches' guild and when I saw him, I thought he had been sent as extra protection." Sarah shook her head sadly. "He had us all fooled. No one knew he'd gone bad. He knocked me out. I should have been able to tell he'd gone bad."

"Well, it all turned out fine in the end and you helped with the spell that got him," Celeste smiled at Sarah.

Sarah nodded. "From the look of things, the witch ghosts had been waiting to get back at him. They knew all along that he'd turned. It took both of us to boost that spell. Your powers are stronger than you think. Well, I'm sure you want to get to the hospital, so I'll be off on my broomstick." She laughed at the sisters' surprised looks. "Just kidding, I walked."

As Sarah left with Raven trotting behind her, Celeste held up the crystal ball. She gazed inside it, but it was dark.

Morgan took the ball and looked into it. "I guess there's not much in our future. This thing isn't showing anything."

"That's probably a good thing," Fiona joked as she bent down, picking up the stones she'd thrown at Henry. "Besides, we have more important things to think about. Jolene is in the hospital and we need to be by her side. And Matteo was hurt very badly."

"First, let's secure this crystal ball," Morgan insisted. "I'll call Luke and tell him we have it. Maybe he can drive down and take it back to Dorian while we stay here until Jolene gets out of the hospital."

"Good idea. I'm anxious to get to the hospital and see her and Mateo," Fiona said as she headed for the door.

"I'm just glad they'll both be okay, but I want to see for myself." Morgan moved to exit the house, but the doorway was suddenly blocked by Peterson. "Did you forget something?" Morgan asked in surprise.

"Yeah, the crystal ball. Hand it over or you'll end up in a lot worse shape than your sister and her boyfriend."

Chapter 22

Morgan clutched the crystal ball to her chest, protecting it instinctively. She stepped back, away from Peterson, her eyes flicking to the one unboarded window. All the other police cars were gone. Only Peterson's car remained. "Crystal ball?" Morgan stalled for time by playing dumb.

Peterson stepped forward and looked down at the ball she held close. "Don't play dumb. You know exactly what I'm talking about."

Morgan saw the truth in a flash. "So, you've known all along. *That's* why you've been following us."

Peterson laughed. "Yeah. You probably just thought I was a dumb cop, huh? I've been watching your every move. I even gave you the clue that sent you here. Dr. Bly told me one of those old witches buried the ball around here and put a spell on the area. I knew I wouldn't be able to get into the house without you, so I had to give you a clue that led you here. I would have been here sooner, but I got tied up. Then again, it gave you the chance to get rid of Henry for me, so it's all good."

Morgan thought about that. Hadn't Henry been the one who'd given them the clue, even if he'd directed them to a different area? *Peterson* had been the one to remind them that Salem Village was a different place back in 1692. He'd known what they were up to all along and that his information would help the search for the relic.

She glanced at Fiona and shifted her hold on the crystal ball in a silent signal that she was going to toss the ball to her. Fiona's eyes narrowed slightly which Morgan hoped meant she understood.

Celeste's eyes widened when she put the pieces together. "Wait a minute. *You* killed Nancy!"

"Yes. I killed her and Opal, too. But they didn't have what I needed. It turns out you ladies did, though I suspected that from the start. Dr. Bly warned me about you. I'm going to collect a mighty big bounty from him when I bring back that crystal ball. It'll be easy peasy, especially now that your most powerful sister is in the hospital and won't be able to fight this." Peterson took a geode from his pocket.

Morgan's fist curled around her obsidian pendant. But the pendant wouldn't help much against the geode. The pendant was more for redirecting energy aimed *at* her. The geode would suck all the paranormal energy *out* of her. She couldn't let that happen.

Jolene had the most powerful paranormal skills for fighting, but as the oldest sister, Morgan saw it as her job to protect the others. It was three against one here and Morgan intended to use her intuition to anticipate his next move, blocking his efforts so the three of them could overtake him. She'd seen Fiona pick up the rocks and knew those could be used to fight Peterson.

In one swift move, Morgan tossed the crystal ball to Fiona and had faith that she would catch it while Morgan focused on using her intuition to outwit Peterson.

Her gut instincts told her that Peterson was going to step forward and to her right so she swung around, stepping to the left and kicking her foot out.

She was rewarded when her foot hit soft flesh.

Peterson grunted and stumbled forward.

Morgan spun around behind him, kicking out toward the hand that held the geode.

Success! The geode tumbled from his hand and bounced on the floor, landing face down which rendered it useless for energy draining. Morgan's elation was short-lived.

Peterson spun back around with a small blue gun in his hand. Morgan recognized it as a smaller version of the energy spewing guns that Dr. Bly was so fond of using and very similar to Henry's gun.

Morgan's heart froze as Peterson aimed the gun directly at her. Her gaze flicked over his shoulder to Fiona, who was reaching in her pocket with her free hand. Morgan knew she was reaching for the stones. A movement on her right pulled her attention from Fiona.

Celeste gave a high karate kick toward Peterson's gun-holding hand.

Peterson was too fast, however. He whirled around, bringing up his knee, blocking Celeste's kick, and kicking back. Celeste dropped to the floor with a thud. Peterson turned back to Morgan, unleashing the stream of ice blue energy from the gun.

Morgan felt like she'd been hit by lightning. The electrical force seized up her lungs then traveled to her arms and legs, effectively paralyzing them. Her body convulsed in sharp spasms as she fell to the floor. She was conscious long enough to feel the jarring impact of her shoulder and hips against the floor boards ... and then everything went dark.

***

Fear shot through Fiona as she watched Morgan's body collapse in a heap. Was she alive? Fiona didn't have time to think about it because Peterson was aiming the gun at her now.

Celeste had recovered from being kicked and was on her feet behind Peterson. Fiona knew she was getting ready to kick out again, but she needed Celeste to take the crystal ball so she could use both hands to fling the stones.

Fiona willed Celeste to look at her and their eyes locked. Fiona's eyes flicked to the ball as she held it out toward Celeste. Celeste nodded and cupped her palms, holding them out in front of her. In one swift move, Fiona tossed the ball in the air over Peterson's head to Celeste.

Peterson tried to catch it, but it was too high. He whirled around and aimed his gun at Celeste.

Fiona had anticipated this move. She pelted him with two burning hot stones. They peppered into his back above his shoulders, scorching his shirt and filling the room with an acrid smell.

"Ahhhh!" The gun clattered to the floor as Peterson whirled back on Fiona.

Fiona dove for the gun.

Peterson dove for the gun.

Their hands both clutched the gun.

Rolling around on the floor in a fight with the much bigger man, Fiona searched in her pocket for more stones while she tried to keep possession of the gun with just one hand.

Peterson was too strong. He pried her fingers open and rolled away with the gun. He got up on one knee and aimed it at her.

Fiona tightened her hand around the stones. They cut into her palm as she wished her most powerful energy into them. When they started to burn her hand, she opened up and flung the stones at Peterson.

The stones left bright red trails as they arced through the air. Peterson's eyes widened as the stones hurtled toward him. He jerked the gun away from Fiona and aimed at the stones.

Fizz. Splat. Sizzle.

The energy from the gun neutralized the stones and they fell harmlessly to the ground.

A victorious smile split Peterson's face as he looked from Fiona to Celeste. His eyes lit on the crystal ball.

Fiona desperately searched the floor for more stones. She had to protect the crystal ball and Celeste. Morgan was out cold. If anything happened to Fiona, Celeste would be alone. She didn't have the paranormal defenses to fight off what Peterson was dishing out, not without Sarah or Mateo to help boost the spell.

"You sisters really know how to put up a fight." Peterson advanced on Fiona. "I see I'll have to take *you* out before I take the ball from your sister."

Fiona backed up and saw that out of nowhere, Belladonna launched herself at Peterson in a blur of white fur.

Peterson jerked the gun in the cat's direction.

"No!" Fiona jumped toward Peterson's hand to deflect the gun.

Peterson turned in her direction and fired, sending white-hot energy into Fiona's stomach.

Fiona doubled over, searing pain shooting up into her chest. She collapsed sideways to the floor. The last thing she saw was Peterson's fist connecting with Belladonna, sending the cat flying toward the fireplace.

***

Panic seized Celeste. Fiona was collapsed onto the floor. Belladonna's paws softened her contact with the fireplace and hopped down to the hearth. Her white fur was tinged gray with ashes, and she staggered from the effort. Celeste's eyes flew back to Peterson.

A maniacal glare lit the man's face as he turned his gun in her direction.

Her mind whirled with ways she could protect herself. Her movements were hampered by the crystal ball. She didn't dare drop it. She had no idea if it would survive such an impact. Karate was out of the question since she was too far away from him. Could she dodge the debilitating energy?

Maybe she could use the crystal ball.

Celeste held the ball up in between her and the mouth of the gun. Peterson's eyes narrowed and she could see seeds of doubt sprouting in his mind.

"You'd better pray you don't hit this crystal ball or it will explode to smithereens." Celeste said the words confidently though she had no idea if that would actually happen.

"Hand it over. You're no match for me." Peterson glanced at Morgan and Fiona motionless on the floor. "Your sisters can't help you."

A feeling of desperation overtook Celeste as she glanced at Morgan and Fiona. Would they regain consciousness soon? She could vaguely see their spirits struggling to come back to consciousness, but she couldn't communicate with them. They were too weak. She focused all her attention on Peterson. She knew she had to stall him until her sisters woke up.

Peterson stepped closer.

Celeste took a step back. "Hold it right there or I'll smash the crystal ball to bits!"

Peterson's eyes narrowed. "You wouldn't do that."

By the fireplace, Belladonna shook off her daze then skulked around the perimeter of the wall.

Relief surged through Celeste when she realized Belladonna hadn't been hurt. But what was the cat up to? If Belladonna could distract Peterson, Celeste could step in and dislodge the gun with a kick.

Peterson's eyes drifted from Celeste's face to the crystal ball.

She figured he was trying to calculate how to get her while not risking the ball.

An evil grin spread across his face as he aimed the barrel of the gun at Fiona. His thumb flipped a switch on the gun and it pulsed from blue to indigo. "She's only knocked out with a light dose of energy. I can finish her off with a juiced up dose. It should fry her like a pigeon on a high wire."

"No!" A bead of sweat formed on Celeste's brow. She looked down at the crystal ball, but it was still dark. If only it would show her what Peterson's next move was, she could try to outmaneuver him.

Something rubbed against her ankle. Belladonna. She willed the cat to go away. She didn't want her to get hurt in the melee of what was about to happen.

A slight breeze ruffled Celeste's hair. Puffs of gray ash swirled on the chimney hearth. Celeste remembered how the witches had come out of that chimney and what they'd done to Henry.

"*Merow.*"

"*Say the spell.*"

Celeste's eyes jerked to the cat at her feet. Had Belladonna just spoken?

No. The words hadn't come from the cat. It was a disembodied voice that sounded like the voice of Sarah's ghost that she'd spoken to at the Rebecca Nurse house.

Celeste looked at the crystal ball. The modern Sarah had said that her ancestor's ghost was freed once the crystal ball was in the right hands, the Blackmoore sisters' hands. Was she free now, and trying to help Celeste?

The spell had worked on Henry, but only with Sarah's help boost it. Would it work if she tried to do it on her own? Celeste remembered the feeling of power that had surged through her when she said the words.

"*Merow!*" Belladonna put her paw on Celeste's foot.

Celeste looked down into Belladonna's ice blue eyes and saw her cat wink. Could Belladonna boost the spell?

"Now!" Peterson yelled.

Celestial saw Peterson's finger twitched on the trigger of the gun. She had to try. Celeste closed her eyes, reached deep into her heart and said:

> *By Water, Earth, Air and Fire,*
> *I ask thee now grant my desire,*
> *Harming none I now decree*
> *This charm is done, so mote it be*

"Have it your way," Peterson snorted.

Celeste opened her eyes in time to see a stream of dark sapphire energy spew from Peterson's gun toward Fiona.

The spell hadn't worked!

But then the energy stopped midstream.

The hairs on Celeste's arms stood on end as the air crackled with electricity. Belladonna let out a guttural growl.

Peterson's face twisted in horror as the sapphire energy backtracked, making its way toward the gun and Peterson. "No!" Peterson dropped the gun, holding his hands up in front of his face to ward off the energy, but it did no good.

The energy hit him with a loud clap like thunder.

His screams filled the air for a split second and then there was silence as his entire body turned to ash and sprinkled over the floor.

***

Celeste stared down in a mix of horror and amazement at the pile of ash. Had *she* done that with the spell?

The spell had worked, even more powerfully than she had hoped. She'd felt the power even when she'd said it without Sarah's boost. It was as if she was meant to say the words.

Her lips curled in a smile. She felt almost giddy. She'd always felt inadequate because she didn't have the same paranormal combative abilities as her sisters and had to depend on them to defend her against bad guys, but she'd done this all by herself.

Or had she? She glanced down at Belladonna who still had a paw on Celeste's foot.

The cat slitted her eyes then turned and flicked her tail. She padded over to Morgan with barely a sniff in the direction of the ash pile. "*Meow*!' Belladonna nudged Morgan's face.

Morgan moaned and gently pushed Belladonna's wet nose away.

Celeste ran over. "Are you okay?"

Morgan sat up, shaking her head. Her right hand shot up to her chest. "I think so. What happened?"

"Peterson shot you with energy."

"Morgan's eyes fell on the crystal ball that Celeste was still clutching. "It's safe! What happened to Peterson?" She asked, craning her neck to look around.

Before Celeste could answer, a groan sounded from the other side of the room. Fiona. Celeste ran to her while Morgan got to her feet. "Fiona, are you okay?"

Fiona rubbed her stomach and grimaced. "I feel like I drank a cup of Mateo's jalapeño hot sauce, but other than that I'm fine. What about you guys?" Fiona looked around the room. "Where's Peterson?"

"*Meow!*" Belladonna sniffed in the direction of the pile of ash, then made a face and backed away.

"What's that?" Morgan asked.

"*That*," Celeste said in wonder, "is Peterson."

Morgan's eyes grew wide in surprise. She looked from Fiona to Celeste. "How long was I out? And what in the world happened?"

Fiona shrugged, glancing at Celeste. "I tried to fight Peterson off, but he shot me with that gun of his. That's the last thing I remember."

Celeste puffed up proudly as her sisters looked to her for an answer. "Well, it turns out I'm not as defenseless as we thought. I simply used the spell and Peterson was reduced to a pile of ash." She kicked the gun away from the ashes. "I guess we should probably take this. Maybe we can make use of it for future assignments."

Morgan bent down and picked the gun up gingerly. "At the very least, I'm sure Dorian Hall will want to inspect it. Might give her some insight into what Dr. Bly is cooking up in his laboratory."

"And what about that?" Celeste gestured toward the geode. It was still face down, looking like any other rock.

"I'm not touching that thing. I say we leave it." Morgan inched away from it.

"Works for me," Celeste said.

"Now what?" Fiona asked. "Should we call the police?"

Celeste looked out the window. "Peterson's car is still out there. They'll wonder what happened to him."

"Yeah, his car is out there and we're in here with a pile of ash," Morgan said. "How are we going to explain that?"

"I don't think we need to," Celeste said.

"But our fingerprints are all over the place. The police will know we've been here, and with Peterson's car abandoned and that pile of ash ..." Fiona glanced at the pile. "I wonder if they can even figure out that *that* was Peterson."

"They already know we were here," Celeste pointed out. "They don't need to know that we stayed and tangled with Peterson."

"Good point," Morgan added. "In fact, they'd expect us to be rushing off to the hospital to see Jolene and Mateo. Which I suggest we do right after securing the crystal ball."

"Well, if you're sure." Fiona glanced back uneasily at the ashes.

"I'm sure." Morgan's face took on the look it did when she was dialing up her instincts. She smiled and nodded. "In fact, I'm positive there won't be any evidence of what happened between us and Peterson in this house tonight.

Morgan opened the door and a gust of wind whooshed in, blowing the pile of ash straight into the hearth and up the chimney.

Celeste looked back over her shoulder as she followed her sisters and Belladonna out the door. "I guess you're right. It looks just like it did when the police left. No one will ever know what happened in here."

Chapter 23

The persistent beeping was driving Jolene crazy. She tried to block her ears with her hands but only her left hand moved. The other one was secured by ... something. Something warm and comforting.

Where was she? Her eyes didn't want to open, but her body was telling her she was comfortable, lying on something cushiony that smelled like ... rubbing alcohol?

A hospital?

Her eyes flew open.

She *was* in a hospital. And sitting next to her holding her hand was Mateo. Relief flooded through her as memories of what had happened in Sam Gooding's house surfaced. "You're alive!"

"Thanks to you." Mateo brought her knuckles up to his lips and kissed them. "You saved my life with your own energy, almost killing yourself in the process. Now you are a part of me. Forever."

"That sounds like a proposal," Morgan leaned against the doorframe of Jolene's room.

Jolene's brows tugged together in confusion. "Proposal? I don't think so." Why wasn't that thought as disturbing as it should be? Another thought hit Jolene. "The scrying ball? What happened to it?"

"Don't worry." Fiona appeared in the doorway next to Morgan. "It's safe."

"In fact, Dorian Hall herself is coming down to retrieve it and to make sure it gets secured in her secret paranormal vault," Morgan said with a smile.

"She has a secret paranormal vault?" Jolene pushed herself up into a sitting position. She liked the flash of concern in Mateo's eyes, but gently pushing him away as he hovered over her to help.

Celeste pushed her sisters into the room and filed in behind them. "Well, she didn't exactly *say* that, but where the heck else would she be keeping all the relics?"

"Good point." As her sisters surrounded her bed, warmth flooded through Jolene. Everyone was here and safe. What had happened to Henry? "So you guys captured Henry?" Jolene looked from Fiona to Morgan to Celeste. "What happened?"

Morgan filled her in, telling her all the details of what happened with Henry and then Peterson's surprise return visit.

Jolene was shocked. She hadn't been overly fond of Peterson but he'd had her fooled into thinking he was helping them.

Fiona took over the narrative to describe what happened after Morgan was rendered unconscious. Then Celeste filled in the very end, all that happened after Fiona was out.

"We were a little worried when we got here and you were still out, but the doctor said you'd probably wake up today and with Mateo here watching over you, we knew you were in good hands." Morgan smiled at Mateo.

"Wait a minute." Jolene asked in shock, "You mean I've been asleep for a whole day?"

"Yes. You needed your rest." Mateo squeezed her hand. "You depleted almost all of your energy, though of course the doctors don't explain it quite that way."

"No wonder I'm starving." Jolene let her head flop back against the bed cushion.

Fiona held up a white bag she had in her hand. "I figured you might be. That's why I brought this."

Jolene opened the bag. Inside was a small white container, several plastic spoons and napkins. She laughed. "Finally, that ice cream you owed me." Jolene opened the container and dug her spoon into the creamy deliciousness. She asked Mateo, "How long were you out? What about the gunshot wounds?"

Mateo unbuttoned his shirt, giving them all a view of his muscular chest and three little scars where the shots had been. "Apparently, your spell worked wonders, along with the carnelian stones. The spell boosted the power of them and I healed in a few hours. The doctors actually think these are old wounds from years ago. I was released last night and I've been sitting here watching you ever since."

Her heart melted at the thought of Mateo watching over her, guarding and protecting her while she slept. But she didn't want to say it out loud. She didn't want to make it seem like she *needed* him because that would mean things she wasn't ready to accept.

"So what about Belladonna? Is she okay?" Jolene picked the other spoons out of the bag and handed them around, then passed the ice cream contained to Mateo.

Celeste laughed. "Oh, she's perfectly fine. Persnickety as usual, complaining that we left her in the hotel room."

"And Sarah?" Jolene asked. The foggy memory of Sarah's voice telling her to say the spell surfaced. Mateo had just said that the spell had boosted her power and the power of the carnelians.

"She's fine." Fiona took the ice cream container from Mateo.

Jolene asked, still trying to get everything straight in her muddled head, "So Peterson and Henry were both working for Bly?"

Morgan shook her head. "Peterson was, but Henry was on his own. He was actually a member of the witch community. He has some low-level paranormal powers and had been mining witch intelligence for years to try and find the crystal ball."

"What was he planning on doing with it?" Jolene asked.

Morgan shrugged as she licked ice cream off her spoon. "Money. Power. Same things Dr. Bly wants to use it for, I imagine."

"So Peterson knew from the start that we had the scrap of paper that the killer had left in Nancy's hand," Jolene mused aloud. "Because he was the killer. He found out he'd left a scrap behind, but it was gone when he got back there. We were the only ones on the scene, so we had to have it."

"But it wasn't that obvious something had been in Nancy's hand. If he'd accused us outright, it might have tipped us off that he was the killer," Morgan said.

"I never noticed he had the same energy trail as the killer because when I raised my awareness at Amity's place, we knew the killer had already been there, so I couldn't differentiate it from Peterson's. And I couldn't even get a reading at Opal's," Jolene said. "I never tried to read him any other time, unfortunately."

"So, you're finally awake." Cassiopeia's voice drifted in from the doorway. She sauntered into the room, favoring Mateo with a wide smile.

Jolene could see the affection pass between them. They were as close as she was with her sisters. The sisters parted to make room for her.

Cassiopeia held up a familiar burlap bag as she took her place next to Jolene's bed. "I believe this is yours." She held the bag out to Fiona.

"Thank you! But how did you get it?" Fiona took the bag, peering eagerly inside.

Cassiopeia waved her hand. "As president of the witches' guild, I have certain ... opportunities. Anyway, it is yours by rights, so I don't think Henry will complain if he finds it missing."

Morgan looked at Cassiopeia sharply. "Oh, is he better?"

Cassiopeia shook her head. "No. Henry made a big mistake and I don't think he'll be 'better' any time soon. He certainly won't be welcome at any guild meetings ever again."

"Well, I sure can't blame you there," Celeste said.

"And I heard the police found evidence linking Peterson to the murders of Opal Mines and Nancy Baumann, so they aren't surprised that he's disappeared," Cassiopeia said.

Morgan frowned. "How do you know that?"

"Oh, I have my sources in the Salem P.D." Cassiopeia turned to Mateo. "Turns out you were right. It's a good thing we gave them the spell. Otherwise, I hear you may not be with us, dear brother."

Jolene mulled that over. She did vaguely remember saying the words of the spell. But was that really what caused her to be able to save Mateo? And had Celeste's chanting of the spell really caused the witch ghosts to attack Henry and the energy to incinerate Peterson ... or had they both had that magical ability within them the whole time?

"That's true." Mateo tugged on Jolene's hand, pulling her out of her thoughts. When she looked at him, he asked. "So, *now* do you believe in witches?"

"Well, I'm not exactly sure. I mean it *seemed* like the spell did make things more powerful, but I need more evidence."

Cassiopeia rolled her eyes. "See, I told you she wouldn't believe."

Mateo patted Jolene's hand. "That's okay. She will soon enough. And I owe her my life, so I'm making it my business to personally coach her until she believes."

Personally coach her? Did that mean he was going to stick around? Jolene might be able to warm up to that idea, but she still couldn't bring herself to admit it. She shrugged and said, "I don't know what I believe."

Mateo leaned back in his seat and took the container of ice cream that Celeste passed to him. "Fine by me. I've got plenty of time to prove it to you."

Jolene settled back in her bed. In a few minutes, she'd insist on someone finding her clothes and start pestering the nurses to discharge her, but for now she wanted to revel in the success of another job well done.

The scrying ball was safe and no one close to her had been harmed. They'd even made new friends in Cassiopeia and Sarah, though Cassiopeia *was* kind of pushy about the spells. Yet, Jolene had to admit that it *did* appear as if the spell had helped them out, especially Celeste.

She still wasn't sure if she believed in spells or witches. It might take someone a very long time to convince her of either. But with Mateo doing the convincing ... well, what could be wrong with it taking a long time? Maybe even a long, long time.

A girl could wish, couldn't she?

The end.

Sign up for my newsletter and get my latest releases at the lowest discount price:

_http://www.leighanndobbs.com/newsletter

If you want to receive a text message on your cell phone when I have a new release, text COZYMYSTERY to 88202 (sorry, this only works for US cell phones!)

Want more Blackmoore Sister's adventures? Buy the rest of the books in the series For Your Kindle:

Dead Wrong (Book 1)
Dead & Buried (Book 2)
Dead Tide (Book 3)
Buried Secrets (Book 4)
Deadly Intentions (Book 5)
A Grave Mistake (Book 6)

A Note From The Author

I hope you enjoyed reading this book as much as I enjoyed writing it. This is the seventh book in the Blackmoore sisters mystery series and I have a whole bunch more planned!

The setting for this book series is based on one of my favorite places in the world - Ogunquit Maine. Of course, I changed some of the geography around to suit my story, and changed the name of the town to Noquitt but the basics are there. Anyone familiar with Ogunquit will recognize some of the landmarks I have in the book.

The house the sisters live in sits at the very end of Perkins Cove and I was always fascinated with it as a kid. Of course, back then it was a mysterious, creepy old house that was privately owned and I was dying to go in there. I'm sure it must have had an attic stuffed full of antiques just like in the book!

Today, it's been all modernized and updated —I think you can even rent it out for a summer vacation. In the book the house looks different and it's also set high up on a cliff (you'll see why in a later book) where in real life it's not. I've also made the house much older to suit my story.

Also, if you like this book, you might like my Mystic Notch series which is set in the White Mountains of New Hampshire and filled with magic and cats. You can find out more about this series on my website.

This book has been through many edits with several people and even some software programs, but since nothing is infallible (even the software programs) you might catch a spelling error or mistake and, if you do, I sure would appreciate it if you let me know - you can contact me at lee@leighanndobbs.com.

Oh, and I love to connect with my readers so please do visit me on facebook at http://www.facebook.com/leighanndobbsbooks or at my website http://www.leighanndobbs.com.

Are you signed up to get notifications of my latest releases and special contests? Go to: http://www.leighanndobbs.com/newsletter and enter your email address to signup - I promise never to share it and I only send emails every couple of weeks so I won't fill up your inbox.

About the Author

USA Today best selling Author, Leighann Dobbs, has had a passion for reading since she was old enough to hold a book, but she didn't put pen to paper until much later in life. After a twenty-year career as a software engineer with a few side trips into selling antiques and making jewelry, she realized you can't make a living reading books, so she tried her hand at writing them and discovered she had a passion for that, too! She lives in New Hampshire with her husband, Bruce, their trusty Chihuahua mix, Mojo, and beautiful rescue cat, Kitty.

Find out about her latest books and how to get discounts on them by signing up at:

http://www.leighanndobbs.com/newsletter

Connect with Leighann on Facebook
http://facebook.com/leighanndobbsbooks

More Books By Leighann Dobbs:

Mystic Notch
Cats & Magic Cozy Mystery Series
* * *

Ghostly Paws
A Spirited Tail
A Mew To A Kill
Paws and Effect

Mooseamuck Island
Cozy Mystery Series
* * *

A Zen For Murder
A Crabby Killer

Kate Diamond
Adventure/Suspense Series
* * *

Hidden Agemda
Ancient Hiss Story

<u>*Blackmoore Sisters*</u>
<u>*Cozy Mystery Series*</u>
* * *

Dead Wrong
Dead & Buried
Dead Tide
Buried Secrets
Deadly Intentions
A Grave Mistake

<u>*Lexy Baker Cozy Mystery Series*</u>
* * *

Lexy Baker Cozy Mystery Series Boxed Set
Vol 1 (Books 1-4)

Or buy the books separately:

Killer Cupcakes (Book 1)
Dying For Danish (Book 2)
Murder, Money and Marzipan (Book 3)
3 Bodies and a Biscotti (Book 4)
Brownies, Bodies & Bad Guys (Book 5)
Bake, Battle & Roll (Book 6)
Wedded Blintz (Book 7)
Scones, Skulls & Scams (Book 8)
Ice Cream Murder (Book 9)
Mummified Meringues (Book 10)

Brutal Brulee (Book 11 - Novella)

<u>*Contemporary Romance*</u>

* * *

Sweet Escapes
Reluctant Romance

Made in the USA
San Bernardino, CA
07 December 2017